SUDDENLY SHE WAS CLINGING TO HIM MINDLESSLY. . .

In her ears, his deep voice sounded softly. Then his mouth slid to her throat in subtle caresses. One hand slipped the thin strap of her nightgown down as it stroked the satiny skin of her shoulder.

Instinctively, her own hands betrayed her, reaching up to find the strong column of his neck, her fingers seeking his thick dark hair. A ripple of excitement went through him; she felt him tense against her. Then his gentle, searching hand moved downward over the opulent curve of her breast. . . .

CANDLELIGHT ECSTASY ROMANCES™

STOLEN HOLIDAY

Marjorie Eatock

A CANDLELIGHT ECSTASY ROMANCE™

Published by
Dell Publishing Co., Inc.
1 Dag Hammarskjold Plaza
New York, New York 10017

Dell ® TM 681510, Dell Publishing Co., Inc.

Candlelight Ecstasy Romance™ is a trademark of
Dell Publishing Co., Inc., New York, New York.

ISBN: 0-440-17742-1

Printed in the United States of America

First printing—January 1982

Dear Reader:

In response to your enthusiasm for Candlelight Ecstasy Romances™, we are now increasing the number of titles per month from three to four.

We are pleased to offer you sensuous novels set in America depicting modern American women and men as they confront the provocative problems of a modern relationship.

Throughout the history of the Candlelight line, Dell has tried to maintain a high standard of excellence, to give you the finest in reading pleasure. It is now and will remain our most ardent ambition.

Editor
Candlelight Romances

To Lita, Sandy, Edith, Debbie, Kathy,
Sherol, Anita, the two Janes
and especially Boo,
who all like a
"nice romance"

CHAPTER I

Jane gasped. She felt as if she were drowning—felt it as hopelessly as though real waters were surging up over her head.

In a thin voice she repeated after her fiancé, "Your *mother* thinks we should honeymoon in Las Vegas!"

Howard answered calmly. "Mother says Niagara isn't smart anymore."

He took a forkful of dietetic cottage cheese, measured it with his eye, dropped a curd back onto the plate, then added, "Besides, Mother has never been to Las Vegas."

Then Jane knew it was true, knew she *was* drowning.

"*Your mother* is going with us on our honeymoon?"

"Of course. She can get a ten percent discount through her travel club." Howard looked up from his fork to his staring wife-to-be. Completely misinterpreting the stare, his smooth, plump cheeks pinkened. In haste he appended, "Naturally we'll have separate rooms."

Looking back much later, Jane would realize that the blush had been the catalyst—the blush which, for Howard, was a full-fledged, hot-breathed leer.

But for the moment all Jane could think of was that the waters had indeed closed over her head. She was drowned, washed up on shore, beached, and finished—and she was only twenty-two years old! Howard and his mother were going to put her in a neat box and she was going to buried alive for the rest of her life.

Something stirred inside her, something that began to struggle, to protest like a crying child: *But I just escaped from a box!*

Perhaps it wasn't fair to call her own mother's long illness and death a box. She had loved her widowed mother dearly and had not resented one of those five years of constant daily care. Her mother's entire life had been wrapped up in her "little girl," and Jane had returned that devotion.

Nonetheless, at that critical moment of Jane Doorn's existence, all metaphors were a little blurred. On a rising tide of frightening truth she looked at Howard for the first time clearly and was aghast—at him, at herself, at what she was allowing to happen.

Another box! With Howard in it! Howard and his corsetted, gimlet-eyed mother! Howard and his mother and all the things so vital to them—credit ratings, important ancestors, name-brand groceries, and proper schools for the children!

Jane dropped her eyes to her plate. She couldn't look at him any longer lest he see the revulsion in her gaze. She carefully forked up the last bits of her Luncheon Special trying vainly to transform chilling panic into some sort of calm rationale.

Howard Van Tassel was a "good thing." Her mother had thought so, had urged her into the engagement, saying, "He'll look after you when I'm gone, Jane." Having her daughter looked after had been very important to Jane's mother. A quiet, fat, studious child, Jane had graduated from high school with scholastic honors and gone directly into a steady job keeping books for Elbert Electronics. She'd had no contact with what Mrs. Doorn had considered the real world—which was full of wicked men that Mrs. Doorn knew through her soap operas were just waiting to ruin a good girl!

"Believe me, Janey," she'd murmured many, many times, "Mother *knows.*"

But Mother was gone now. And Janey, finally shaking off the numb fog of grief, had just seen the good thing with clear eyes.

No longer did she see the rising young banker whose home, car, and boat were the envy of lesser executives, to whom store clerks toadied and inferiors gave up their parking places. Before her now was the fussy, pampered, only child of a possessive mother who rose early each morning to personally cook his oatmeal and lay out his clothes—an overfed baby of nearly thirty who was already letting his body turn to soft flab—a man who in six short weeks meant to take her, Jane Doorn, into his life—and his bed till death do them part.

How inconsequential were his physical weaknesses. How

small against real estate and assets, country club membership and an executive position in the Junior League.

Yet, to Jane, they were suddenly—and perhaps irrevocably—monumental. Rash, improvident girl that she was, she discovered herself clinging to her chair with her fingernails to keep from running away!

Howard never noticed. He was not a perceptive young man except when it came to money.

He reached over, took a bit of the frosting from his fiancée's untouched cake, and popped it into his mouth. He touched the baby silk of his fair moustache delicately with a napkin, folded the linen neatly, picked up the check, and frowned.

"Did you order bleu cheese for your salad?" he asked.

"Yes." The answer was barely a whisper.

"They charge extra for bleu cheese."

"I'm sorry," she said, and loathed herself. He barely noticed. The small pocket calculator came out. With a careful finger he figured the tip, put the calculator away, and counted change from his coin purse.

"There," he said, standing up and straightening his vest over the slight bulge above his belt buckle. "That will do. The rolls were stale anyway. I don't think this is quite what the Booster Club is looking for."

"The—Booster Club?"

"To hold their monthly luncheon." He was making a neat check by the restaurant's name in a tidy notebook. "No, indeed."

So that was why he'd brought her here! Not because he wanted to take his fiancée to a nice café! Not because it was the second anniversary of their engagement—which he obviously hadn't remembered anyway!

Sublimely unaware of the shock wave inside his fiancée's plainly coiffed head (Mother didn't approve of expensive hair styles), Howard bent with a waft of aftershave, and discreetly pecked Jane's cheek. "I have to go. Remember—if that check from McIlhenny and McIlhenny comes to you, bring it right over. We need to get your mother's medical bills settled."

Jane didn't look up. "All right."

Reassured, he added, "And don't forget, this is Mother's bridge club night. She needs us for a table."

"Howard—must we?"

"Must we what?"

"Play bridge? Sally says there's a good movie at the theater."

He frowned, partly because Jane's coworker Sally smoked, roller-discoed, and liked Waylon Jennings. Howard deplored Waylon Jennings.

A little severely he answered, "Mother *expects* us. Good-bye, Jane."

"Good-bye, Howard."

The words echoed in her head like tennis balls bouncing off an empty building: Good-bye, Howard . . . good-bye, Howard. . . .

An idea formed that made her almost dizzy with fright. She watched him go—a plump little gamecock smiling benignly at the other diners, who waved or spoke or fawned, depending on the size of their involvement with Howard's bank.

The deference extended to her too. All over town people kow-towed—at the grocery, the gas station, the department stores. They always would—as long as she was engaged to Howard.

Or married to him.

In a box with him, the lid legally fastened down, her horizon limited to Howard forever and ever. . . .

A sheen of perspiration shone on Jane's smooth forehead, and she gripped her fingers together to keep them from shaking.

She must be out of her mind. What she was thinking was impossible, wild, fantastic. It couldn't be done. She'd never have the courage, never in this world—not dull, obedient Jane. That tiny diamond on her finger meant a commitment, and Doorns never went back on commitments.

But! said that strange voice inside her brain again. *But one little adventure, Jane—one small piece of excitement before you're boxed. What harm would it do?*

You have the money. You know you have. It's not much, but it's all yours. Take it, Jane. Take it and run.

Before it's too late . . .

"It's already too late."

She'd said the words out loud. The passing waitress glanced at her curiously, and hesitated. "Ma'am?"

Crimson, Jane shook her head, and, very embarrassed, began to fumble with her coat and bag. The waitress shrugged and moved on. Then, half out of the chair, Jane's eye fell on her denuded cake. Slowly she sat down again, staring at it. Somewhere inside her a small cinder of anger began to glow.

He hadn't even asked for the frosting. Perhaps she might have felt different if he had asked. Maybe then that small cinder might not have been fanned by rising indignation.

Suddenly she found herself thinking the incredible thought that she had to get away—just for a little while. She would come back and marry Howard—but right now she *had to get away!*

The small voice had done a turnaround; it was playing devil's advocate, jeering, *You'll never do it! Never in this world! You're too chicken!*

She would! She would do it!

Her jawline set, Jane scrambled to her feet, gathered her coat and bag, and started to walk away.

She stopped, looked back, and went back. She picked up her own neatly folded napkin and crumpled it into a ball—a mundane act that for Jane signified a declaration.

She also swept Howard's niggling change into her bag and recklessly dropped a dollar bill in its place. It was her last dollar, but she knew how to remedy that—if she had the nerve. Shrugging into her sensible, four-year-old cloth coat, she stepped out into the cold, snowy street and grimly turned her steps toward the bank.

It was like the games she and her mother had played when she was a child. The players always started on square one. That's where she was now—square one.

Howard, already closeted with a client, was surprised to see Jane go by. She hadn't mentioned coming to the bank—and if she didn't hurry she'd be late getting back to work. Howard disapproved of being late. "Punctuality is the cornerstone of discipline," his mother always said.

His client asked, "Who was that?"

"Jane Doorn," Howard answered.

"Katrine Doorn's daughter? I didn't recognize her. She's lost her baby fat."

"Some time ago," Howard answered absently. Watching Jane, he almost wished he'd gone ahead and bought that silky blue negligee for Jane's Christmas present. But of course, as Mother had said, the flannel bathrobe was much more sensible.

"How's she fixed?" the client asked.

Howard came back to earth. "I beg your pardon?"

But his client was both elderly and obtuse. "Fixed! Fixed! At one time Katrine owned a bundle of land out where the expressway is going through."

That was one topic Howard had absolutely no wish to discuss. Quickly he said, "Ah, well, you know how those things are. Now, about the interest charges . . ."

The male teller in the end cage, being at leisure and a bachelor, watched Jane's approach with sudden interest.

Holy smoke, he thought, *what's happened to our Jane today? She looks almost alive! In fact, get rid of the mud-colored hair and the potato-bag coat and she might not be half bad. . . .*

Unaware that her hair and coat were being maligned, Jane was concentrating on approaching the teller in question. She'd seen Howard's surprised glance and now her heart was pounding thunderously in her ears. The cranberry in her usually plain cheeks was more than wind whip.

Desperately she told herself, *It's my money,* and shoved her passbook under the grill so hard it almost skidded onto the floor.

"I want to take out a thousand dollars," she said, and could hardly believe the croaky voice was hers.

Startled, the teller asked, "You mean transfer it to checking, Jane?"

"No. No—I want cash."

Surely the word "cash" was echoing off the rafters, she

thought. Surely the entire bank had turned and was looking at this totally mad Jane Doorn, gripping the fake marble of the counter with tense fingers and asking for a thousand dollars in cash!

As a matter of fact, the teller had barely heard her, and it was taking all his training to mask his surprise. He'd never known Jane to write a check for any more than fifty—other than bills, of course.

Blandly his hands transacted the business while he peered with curiosity from spectacled eyes. "Hey," he said with heavy humor as he counted out five stacks of twenties, two hundred dollars in a stack, "let's go to Las Vegas, you and me."

The words *Las Vegas* seemed to have a strange effect on Jane. She drew in a sharp breath, and her eyes almost flashed. "Do we have to take your mother?"

"You must be kidding!" He rubber-banded the bundle, gave it a parting pat, and watched her stuff the wad nervously into her purse. "Anyway, don't get mugged before you spend it."

"Even getting mugged," she answered grimly, "would be a change. Where do I sign?"

"Here." He pointed with a rubber-tipped finger. The remark about the change had lost him.

She put down the pen and nodded. "Thanks," she said and her voice sounded as if she were catching a cold. Glancing almost wildly around the bank, she clutched her bag and headed for the door. She was just a speck away from running, the teller realized as he listened to her heels clicking on the pseudo-terrazzo. *What the hell,* he thought, unconsciously echoing Jane, *it's her money.*

The boss, he noted, waved and beckoned. But Jane shook her head and whizzed right by. The clock began to strike the hour. Jane would be late to work, both men thought. But Howard couldn't see what the teller saw—that Jane Doorn did not turn right toward Elbert Electronics, but went right on down the wind-blustered street toward home.

It was only four blocks and she never minded walking—exercise being one of her weapons in the war against baby fat. Howard also approved of walking; he meant to sell her mother's car after they were married, and keeping the mileage low would bring a better sale.

But today Jane did mind walking. Not only was it blustery cold, but she also felt very conspicuous. She was certain the people she met could read the guilt in her face and sense the wad of money in her bag.

But it was her money! She had every right to carry it if she wished! The guilt she felt was ridiculous.

What I am really feeling, she told herself unhappily, *is the weight of Howard's disapproval.*

Well, he'd just have to disapprove.

Yet, despite her brave words, her cold feet slowed almost involuntarily.

What was she doing? What in the world was she doing? Had she taken leave of her senses?

Turn around, Jane, she told herself. *You still can. Go to work. Put the money back. You can. There's time. . . .*

Ahead of her down the block, a car crunched to the slushy curb. Betty Gray got out, followed by her tall boyfriend. He swung Betty up into his big arms, kissed her enthusiastically, put her down, pinched her fanny, and said, "I love you. See you tonight." Then he got back into his car and drove away.

He went right by Jane without noticing her. As Jane reached Betty, Betty said self-consciously, "Hi. Isn't he awful?"

But Betty was smiling as she went up to her house taking the steps at a skip.

"Awful," echoed Jane.

Howard had never said "I love you." They'd not really talked about love. And although he'd certainly attempted numerous other intimacies, pinching her fanny on a public street was not within Howard's scope.

Jane wasn't aware she'd stopped, that she was standing motionless in the snow, her purse clutched to her dowdy coat, the wind blowing her hair across her tense face.

Glancing back to Jane as she closed the door, Betty noted her mood but thought nothing of it. Janey Doorn was nice, but dull.

A good girl, she said to herself and grinned. She remembered

16

Mrs. Van Tassel saying sententiously to her own mother, "I thank the Lord every day that my Howard is marrying a good girl."

"Ich," said Betty of Howard Van Tassel, and let it go at that.

Out on the sidewalk a sudden blast of snow needled Jane's face, bringing her out of her trance. But the image remained, etched into the back of her mind: Betty bear-hugged in her Tony's arms. What did it matter that he was only a Severetti from Mill Road, that he had dropped out of high school and would never be more than a laborer for some construction outfit? He had said "I love you" out loud on a public street.

Jane glanced up and down that street. Narrowed against the frost, her eyes found each house, each tree, each shrub, even the lampposts as familiar as her own hand. Somewhere there were different houses, different trees, different people—people to whom she could be a new girl with money looking for a good time. That's what she was *going* to be—just for a while—just for a while, Howard . . .

She could glimpse her own house far down the block. Almost blindly she trudged toward it. As it grew closer, her footsteps quickened. Suddenly she had an urgent need to hurry. By the time she reached the porch she was running.

CHAPTER II

A vestige of common sense slowed Jane down at the door lest the neighbors think her crazy. She made herself go through the routine of taking the mail from the box. Stamping snow from her feet, she riffled through the assortment. Her actions were automatic until she came to a long, thin envelope with McIlhenny and McIlhenny as the return address. A conditioned response took over and she stuck the envelope in the top of her bag to take to Howard.

Then a sliver of reality nicked the haze: *Whoa! You're not going to see Howard!*

Another inner voice took it up—a cunning, reasonable voice determined not to be robbed of its fun: *Of course you are—just not for a few days. Howard can wait!*

Jane found herself transfixed, staring at the morning newpaper but seeing Howard's incredulous face, hearing his voice say, "You're going to *what?*"

Jane gulped and broke the spell. But she was left weak-kneed, knowing full well that she couldn't face him. Not now. She was going to have to sneak out of town and do the facing when she got back or she'd never go. Under the bombarding crush of Howard's horrifying logic she'd flatten like a pricked balloon. No one could make her feel more guilty and ungrateful than Howard.

And I hate it! she thought angrily.

She almost said the words out loud. They echoed in her head: *I hate it! I hate it!*

Her jaw thrust forward ominously, Jane unlocked the door and went into the warm living room. As usual, it smelled of dry wood and aging tapestry. As she bent to spread the newspaper for her wet boots, the slight hitch in the thrum of the furnace motor told her once more she'd be lucky to make spring without a whale of a repair bill.

19

She'd dropped one boot when a headline caught her eye: DANCER DISAPPEARS! The story ran on. "Crystal Bell's agent says she is exhausted, needs rest and quiet. 'Even fame can wear you out,' he reports."

Jane's reply to that was to drop her other boot. She had no sympathy or time for some pampered pussycat in a leotard. What she did have was the problem of calling Elbert Electronics and giving them some reason for not being there for a week.

She looked at her reflection in the old mirror with its faded gilt ribands. She was biting her lip.

Well she might. What was she going to say?

She'd say she was sick. No. She wouldn't lie about it. What then? The truth.

But what was the truth?

I'm running away. I'm going to buy some clothes and see some shows and try to have a big enough splurge to last me the rest of my life.

How awful it sounded, put in words like that—how shallow, how childish, greedy, thoughtless, and irresponsible!

The damning words tumbled through her brain. She couldn't do it! How could she even have thought of such a thing? But it wasn't too late. . . . She could go on to work, put the money back tomorrow. . . .

Then the phone began to ring. From the silent kitchen with its cold, faded linoleum it trilled out, echoed by the more ladylike bell at what had been her mother's bedside.

Jane stood frozen to the spot.

What if it was Howard? Of course he'd seen her in the bank. By now he probably knew she'd withdrew a thousand dollars. What could she say to him? How could she explain?

She closed her eyes, gritted her teeth, and tried to think, but the tinny shrilling bounced from the walls, filled her ears, stretched her nerves until she suddenly found herself screaming, "Stop it! Stop it!"

It stopped.

Appalled, she opened her eyes and looked around. Everything

was the same, but now the silence was worse than the noise. It closed in on her with velvet, smothering hands.

Complete panic took over. She ran like a rabbit for her bedroom with its neat pink dresser set, its row of Great Classics of Literature, and its ruffled curtains. She did own a suitcase. She'd bought it once when she'd thought she was going on a three-day weekend with Sally and another girl at the office—a weekend her mother had quashed with vigor when she'd discovered Sally *drank*. Jane tumbled her suitcase off the closet shelf, threw in a load of underclothes and pajamas, some double-knit pants and tops, a cardigan sweater, and a slacks-skirt-jacket combination that the mail-order catalog called "weekender"—the kind that with a scarf or pin the elegant young lady transforms into six different and smashing new outfits. Only Jane never had. On Jane they'd always looked unmistakably like the same slacks or skirt or jacket.

She stopped.

Gritting her teeth again, she suddenly dumped everything out all over the bed. No! She wasn't taking those clothes. None of it.

If she was going to be hanged for a lamb, she may as well be hanged for the whole damned sheep—or however that saying went!

A few moments later Jane emerged from the bedroom carrying a suitcase that contained only a paperback Agatha Christie and her mother's good pearls. She scooped up her wet boots from the newspaper, snapped the lock on the front door, and turned down the thermostat. There were cold loafers by the kitchen sink. She shoved colder feet into them. The kitchen opened onto the garage. Her mother's car loomed like a big beetle in the pale light through dusty windows. She threw boots, paper, and suitcase into the backseat, and pushed up the overhead door, letting in cold and blue-white sunshine that made her blink.

The car started obediently. It was a good car, the last thing her dad had bought before he'd died seven years ago. She backed out through a shelf of snow, almost getting stuck in her haste. Feeling the useless spin of back tires, a little common sense came

21

through the panic. She eased up, turned the wheel, and nursed the car out into the street.

In the house the telephone began ringing again. She heard it as she banged down the garage door.

She ran for the car, getting her loafers full of snow, slid onto the cold seat, and shoved the gear into drive.

As she approached the intersection, she suddenly saw a car like Howard's stopped at the red light. Her heart leaped into her throat. She wrenched the wheel, whipped into an alley, and almost drove up the back of a garbage truck. A man yelled "Hey!" indignantly, saving himself by inches. In Jane's mind a near-miss was acceptable. She fishtailed her car on around another corner; then, taking side streets, she routed herself past the municipal windmill, the enormous, tulip gardens, through the high school parking lot, out an obscure avenue and up a little-used ramp to the Interstate. Only then did she feel safe from capture.

Only then. Except—where was she going?

The ramp took her to the eastbound side. All right, that would do. At the edge of town on the interchange was a truck stop. She'd make up her mind there.

Okay, she told herself, okay, Jane. One square at a time. That way you can always go back.

Minutes later, flashing neon lights and rows of parked freight-liners smudging the cold air with their exhaust marked the way station. Jane threaded through them to a vacant pump beneath an enormous metal canopy. A stocking-capped attendant busy with a Chevy glanced over as she rolled down the window.

"Ma'am?" he asked.

"Fill it. Is there a telephone?"

He gestured over his shoulder. She climbed out. She had to tell someone something if she didn't want people out looking for her. But who? And what?

She couldn't risk calling Howard. It may as well be Sally.

She inserted a dime and dialed. At the familiar voice, "El-bert's," overlaid by a gentle mist of Waylon Jennings's familiar

22

baritone, she smiled a little. Sally's eight-track was going, which meant Mr. Elbert had gone to lunch.

"Sally, this is Jane."

"Your boyfriend's looking for you, sweetie," Sally said. "I told him you'd eloped with the guy from the other bank."

Howard must have adored that remark, Jane thought. She swallowed. "Oh, dear," she said with what she hoped was convincing dismay. "He hasn't got my message. Call him back, will you, Sally? Tell him I'm taking those few days off we talked about—going to do some shopping and, oh, you know—I'll be in touch. The Martin file is done. Put it on Mr. Elbert's desk. Thanks. I'll send you a postcard. 'Bye!"

She slammed down the receiver as though it were burning her and scuttled back to her car in full retreat, her cheeks hot. Lies! Out and out lies! And so easily said!

She was both appalled at herself, and pleased; and as her heart stopped thumping, she was also vaguely relieved. Sally hadn't believed a word, of course. Sally knew her too well. Still, she was surely enough of a friend to repeat her message verbatim to Howard. He would be furious, naturally, but the message would save his pride if he'd let it—which he would do all right. She could almost hear him now, nodding, saying, "Yes, yes, a little vacation . . . Jane took her mother's death hard, you know."

He'd cover for himself, and thereby cover for her, too, so that when she came back . . .

Jane shivered.

The stocking-capped attendant said kindly, "Get in your car, ma'am. I'll pump. Turn the heater on and get warm."

She nodded and obeyed. Her loafers were soaked. She peeled them off, reached into the back for the newspaper with the boots on it, donned the dry boots, put the newspaper on the floor for the loafers and, in so doing, turned the paper over. From the bottom half of the front page a rather smudged picture of Crystal Bell looked up. Jane gave it a cursory glance. Smashing legs, of course, lots of dark hair, and considerable cleavage.

At least I could manage the cleavage, Jane thought idly. Her ample bosom had been a source of embarrassment to her mother.

Mrs. Doorn, in fact, had kept Jane in jumpers and shirtwaists until she was out of high school.

Then something else caught her eye—a strip ad at the bottom of the page. It showed palm trees and girls in bikinis and it said: "Three glorious days on a tropical island, round trip $500!"

It was like a sign, an omen. Jane's heart bounced. Five hundred dollars was half her money, but if she spent only two hundred on clothes she'd still have three hundred to blow—and she couldn't conceive of spending two hundred just on clothes anyway!

She snatched up the paper, wet gray rags and all, and tore off the bottom strip. Eagerly she read the rest: "Bake out the winter's cold on Limeberry Cove's white sandy beaches. Tour the great houses and sugar mills of yesterday on St. Thomas and St. John. Enjoy the restored beauty of ancient Frederiksted." Then at the very bottom it said LIMEBERRY VACATIONS, INC. and gave a travel agency's number in Quincy, Illinois.

"Bake out the winter's cold on Limeberry Cove's white sandy beaches. . . ." Jane repeated to herself.

She rolled down the window. "How far to Quincy?" she asked the attendant.

"What?"

"How far to Quincy? Quincy, Illinois?"

"Oh." The attendant shrugged and wiped his nose with a cold red hand. "I don't know. Hey, Mac, how far to Quincy?"

The trucker didn't really bother to look. He'd checked the scale as Jane had gone by and rated her a grudging two points; recognized as female.

"About four hours. Take thirty-four to sixty-one, hang a right and follow it down to the bridge across the Mississippi."

Four hours. Jane glanced at her watch. She could get there about five thirty or six. There'd be time left to shop, to get a motel, and perhaps find this travel agency. If it was in a mall, it might still be open.

"Bake out the cold on Limeberry's white sandy beaches . . ."

24

A small thread of excitement began to curl inside her. Did she dare? Did she honestly dare?

"Check your oil?" the attendant asked.

"It's all right."

She didn't know whether it was or not, but she wanted to get going. She paid for her gas, her fingers secretly touching the wad of money beside it. The gas took her last twenty plus some odd change; that plus the dollar bill she'd left as a tip left her absolutely broke until she started spending the thousand.

As she pulled away, the attendant, frowning, said to the trucker, "Listen to that."

"What?"

"That Buick."

They both listened. The trucker whistled. "The lady's got a problem," he said.

"She's gettin' one, anyway. Think she'll make it to Quincy?"

"Maybe. I had a Buick that did that once. Cost me a bundle."

But Jane, with the windows up and the radio tuned to some cheerful Christmas music, heard nothing.

She was on her way to Limeberry Cove, to "bake out winter's cold on white sandy beaches," to visit sugar mills and great houses—whatever they were—and see her first palm tree, all in three glorious days. Only three days! Surely not even Howard could carp at that. At least, not for long. Could he? Perhaps if she didn't spend all the thousand . . .

Then suddenly she was angry all over again.

Jane, you miserable jellyfish! she said to herself. *If you are going to crawfish and wishy-wash, you may as well go home right now!*

You've done nothing wrong! You've been a bit of a coward, but you've always been that; it can't change overnight. You will be back by Christmas and you're going to marry Howard in January. Nothing is really changing. But if you're going to spoil it all by compromising, you had better turn around and save the damned money!

There was an exit coming up. Coming closer.

She drove right by. It was a sort of achievement. One more square in the game.

She stopped once more at a junction store and by topping the tank forced herself into breaking into the thousand dollars. That was another square. With a can of soda beside her and munching on a Snickers bar, she pulled out into traffic again. The sign said, TAYLOR, MISSOURI, 58 MILES. Taylor Missouri, was the turnoff to Quincy. The sun was a rosy red on her right shoulder, but still she was making very good time. A small thread of excitement began to uncurl again.

It was different just to be alone in the Buick, just to drive as she pleased. Once she even noticed the speedometer spiraling into the seventies; in haste she dropped it again. The last thing she needed was a ticket! Yet, though the speed was gone the exhilaration remained.

Jane Doorn was on her own! There was no one to find her motel for her, no one to order her meals, no one to bail her out if she got into trouble! It was scary to think about—but it was fun. And she could handle it. She knew she could.

Something filmy, ephemeral, wafted through her mind from high school lit class—a poem about "I've left, against the long dark night, but one small candle flame . . ." How did that go? She knit brown brows tensely, and after a moment had the rest: "Shall I husband all the light and make it last the game?

"Or shall I let it burn up bright—so they can read my name?"

That was it. That said it all. This headlong dash of hers, this one indulgent flight into freedom with its inevitable end in guilt and recrimination—this was letting her candle "burn up bright." Surely she'd find someone—somewhere—to remember with her —and be glad for her—when she was in the dark again. . . .

There was a motel right at the end of the narrow, crumbling old bridge, looming brightly across the gleaming roll of turgid water. She parked the car, locked it, and carrying her suitcase, went through the dirty snow up the shallow steps into the warm lobby.

There most of her newfound courage left her flat.

The lobby was filled with sleek, fashionably dressed women carrying cocktail glasses and giving each other little hugs of greeting, presenting immaculately enameled cheeks and kissing the air expertly while their male counterparts gave out hearty handshakes. The air was redolent with perfume and echoing with good-humored laughter. A gorgeous blonde with a honey-colored tan sat at a small table labeled TRAVEL ASSOCIATION MEMBERS REGISTER HERE.

Jane made her way among them to the desk, mumbling, "Excuse me. Excuse me." Although glad she'd dropped her wire-rims in her bag, she'd never felt so tacky in her life.

The clerk seemed to share this summation, but she gave Jane a bright, plastic smile.

"May I help you, ma'am?"

The smile crumbled a bit at the corners when Jane admitted that she had no reservation, and was not using a credit card. The clerk noticed that this dowdy broad carried a suitcase that must have been bought in a thrift shop and seemed to be having difficulty signing her name.

Jane, staring at the blank line, was indeed frozen in arrested motion. Name. Name! Oh, God! What if Howard called around and found her here!

A young woman whose growth had virtually been stopped at the age of fourteen does not become twenty-two in a moment's time. And in the last two hours this headlong flight to freedom had grown immensely important to Jane. The idea of its being snatched away made her heart pound.

Blindly she signed the first thing that came into her head. She was halfway back across the crowded lobby, her room key clutched tightly in her hand, before she realized that by the simple act of signing a name she had become, for the moment, Miss Crystal Bell!

Who in the world was Crystal Bell?

Then she remembered: the dancer!

Great! Good thinking, Jane. You'd better hope no one asks you to dance!

Oh, well. It was done. Besides, no one would look for a celebrity here—not in the midwest in winter! And there were probably a number of Crystal Bells. Still, she wished she hadn't.

She pressed the elevator button for three, having failed to notice the lanky gentleman on the bar stool who, nonetheless, had noticed her. He was not in formal dress (the budget for the little travel agency he and his sister were trying to get off the ground did not stretch to tuxedos) but neither had been the plain woman crossing to the elevator. The thought had given him a kindred feeling. He had been nursing his second scotch and cursing the half-baked promotional that had brought him to this wasteland in the first place. His eyes had not fixed on her for any particular reason, but mostly because she stood out against the dazzle of black and white.

He noted her confusion, the nervous way she shifted her large suitcase. *Small town,* he thought idly. *Upstate. Here for a furtive assignation with her lover—a milkman, no doubt, who is not only married (six children) but has a sinus condition. Her name is—of course. Her name is Irene. Irene—something. Who cares? Naturally she's signed "Smith."*

Intrigued with his own nonsense, he lounged over to the desk, leaned on it, and gave the clerk a cozy smile. The clerk, who liked tanned young men in turtleneck sweaters, smiled back.

"Who was that?" the young man asked.

"Sir?"

"The Brown Bag with Feet. Who was it?"

She giggled, and moved just a little so the signature showed: Crystal Bell.

The lanky young man's considerable jaw loosened. "Good God!"

"Sir? Do you know her? The name sounded familiar to me, but I can't—"

"No, no." He cut her off casually, but his gray eyes were serious. "I don't know her."

But I'm certainly going to try! he added to himself.

Having discovered, also, the assigned room number, he returned quite happily to his scotch.

"Crystal Bell," he murmured into his glass. "Son of a gun."

What have I been telling Karen, he thought. *One celebrity would make our little hostel go—one celebrity with money! And here she is, hiding under a Salvation Army potato bag! Furthermore, those jessied dandies in their monkey suits almost stepped on her and she didn't like that. I could see it. . . . Stars like to feel they're special—even in potato bags.*

But I noticed her, he continued a mite fatuously. *And she's mine, boys. All mine.*

CHAPTER III

The room was shag-carpeted in blue with a matching bedspread and draperies and two chairs on either side of a butcher-block table holding a green glass lamp. Jane thought it was nice. She thought the entire room was nice, particularly the painted view of Montenegro on the wall above her bed. The fact, had she known it, that the same view could be found on the walls of countless motels all across the country wouldn't have mattered to her. Jane had been in motels exactly three times, twice before she was ten, and the last occasion six years ago. She and her mother had gone to a distant relative's funeral in Wisconsin. The room had smelt of mice; worse, some men had been having a loud party next door. Jane's mother had shoved a chair beneath their own doorknob and they'd lain awake in absolute terror the entire night.

"Women are so helpless," her mother had said, "against *men.*"

That they had escaped with virtue intact had been almost anti-climactic to Jane. She'd had a worse time escaping the departed's old goat of a bereaved husband, who'd kept pinching her fanny at the graveside.

Still, Jane did not smile as she plopped her suitcase on the bed and sat down in one of the chairs.

In that crowded lobby she'd never felt so much a non-person in her life! It was a bitter feeling. Fiercely she realized that she wanted to look like those women, belong somewhere as those women did. Would half a thousand dollars do it? Was it already a lost cause?

No one had even noticed her. In fact, she'd been jostled, and the man murmuring "Sorry" had not even looked up. She might have been a mouse scuttling to a hole.

But nothing would change unless she changed it herself. She had sense enough to realize that.

She half-turned to see herself in the mirror, looking with cruel eyes.

A plain girl in an old-lady coat looked back with a discontented frown. Good grief! What a loser!

Well, she wasn't willowy, but she wasn't fat either. Her complexion was dull but clear. As for her hair—she fluffed it with her fingers; it stood out in untidy peaks—as for her hair, she'd been cutting it herself, and she admitted she hadn't been successful.

Don't despair, Jane, she thought. *Remember—one square at a time. The next square is a complete overhaul. And for heaven's sake, don't bawl.* Tears were beginning to sparkle in her eyes, tears of worry and guilt and fear. *Get moving!* she admonished herself.

She swallowed, mopped her eyes with a crumpled Kleenex, turned so she could no longer see her defeated image in the mirror, and reached for the telephone directory.

What she needed was a shopping mall, and the Limeberry Cove Travel Agency. They were listed on East Broadway. She'd have to ask where that was.

Presently, buttoned back into the old coat and with some bright red lipstick applied to make her feel braver, Jane went back into the hall. She had a moment of absolute panic when she heard her door click and couldn't remember if she had the room key—but the feel of the big key inside her shoulder bag answered that. Breathing an enormous sigh of relief, she tried to remember where the stairs were. She caught sight of elevator doors just beyond a a plastic bamboo tree. Good. She could cope with elevators.

The doors opened on the main floor with the lobby to the left and the dining room to the right. As she stepped out, she found a busboy stolidly cleaning up broken glass with a small sweeper. He was chinless and acne-ridden and even less prepossessing than she, and she felt no compunction about speaking to him. She wanted to know how to find East Broadway.

He told her in a bored voice. It sounded easy—until she was out on the snowy streets again.

Jane was simply not used to four-lane city driving. However, after a close brush with a laundry truck and going the wrong way on a one-way street for one frightening block, she began to get her bearings.

Still, the young man who had noticed her earlier in the motel lobby was braced for disaster as he followed her down Main Street to the intersection at Twenty-fourth Street, where she made a right turn from a left-hand lane. He'd been getting some gear from his car when he'd caught a glimpse of her leaving in the Buick. As much out of curiosity as cupidity, he had elected to follow—but not to get himself killed! The woman was crazy. She was probably chauffeur-driven most of the time, he reasoned, and she'd better stay that way. She was a menace!

To his relief, she finally turned into a crowded shopping mall, parked her Buick too close to a Chevy and five feet away from a Trans Am, and disappeared inside the largest department store. He made a fast U-turn, aced out a van, punched down his door locks, and dashed after her. By sheer luck he caught a glimpse of the brown bag going into the dress department.

He lounged around for forty-five minutes, hands in pockets, whistling, trying to look like a bored husband. He also amused himself by trying to conjure up the one vague recollection he had of a magazine layout on Crystal Bell. All he could remember were large breasts and a lot of leg—pretty hard to relate to the brown bag. In fact that was why he almost missed her when she suddenly appeared coming out of the dress department.

The plain cloth coat had been replaced by one of soft leather with just enough cranberry lining showing for the bright red lipstick to set his teeth on edge. The clumpy boots were the same, though, and he followed them into a shoe salon. Three boxes of shoes later, he followed high-heeled pumps into a sports loggia, then a formal shop. By this time Jane was fairly staggering under her purchases, but she forged ahead indefatiguably nevertheless. Bemused both by her endurance and the fact that she was paying cash, he finally trailed her through the awesome glass doors of Elizabeth Arden.

Well, now. If what he had been seeing was her basic face,

building it back up to acceptable Crystal Bell standards was going to take time. Good luck, Elizabeth Arden, he thought.

Feeling he needed to regroup somewhat, he retired to a bench by the court fountain for a good smoke and a little cogitation.

Since she'd registered as Crystal Bell, did that mean she was dropping the incognito and wanted to be recognized—or that she was just letting the chips fall as they may? In either case, he'd better be first in line—unless she was here because she already had something hot going with a male yet unseen. In that case, he was sacked before he started, but those were the breaks. Whatever, La Bell was no amateur, even if she did drive a car like a guided missile. After two successful Broadway plays and two unsuccessful marriages, her status was guaranteed. And what a bonanza she'd be for Limeberry Cove!

The crowds surged by, back and forth. Like lemmings, he thought, comfortable with the fact that he had neither wife nor child to shop for. He chatted pleasantly with an elderly gentleman who wore a round "Honey Dew" button on his lapel—which was explained when a chubby little lady trotted up and said, "Honey, do you want to go start the car while I find Mildred?"

He counted the pennies beneath the shimmering surface of a water fountain, and grabbed the corduroy suspenders of a young man of three, who was earnestly endeavoring to steal a few of the pennies, handing him over, protesting volubly, to his distraught parent.

He looked at his watch, heard his stomach growl, and wondered what the hell he thought he was doing anyway. This travel agency job was making him squirrelly; it just wasn't his thing at all. Yet, when a guy's only sister is left widowed with a child to care for and her husband's whole life's work is about to go down the chute, he can't decently desert her. . . .

A stack of packages walked by. The girl on the other side had a ruffle of dark-honey hair, cheeks that matched her red dress and eyes the shade of her soft brown leather coat.

Holy smoke, he said silently in a solemn tribute to the cosmetologist's art. It was the brown bag.

34

He had to admit, he conceded, following her car's erratic course back to the motel, that his self-appointed task now loomed a bit more pleasant. Except . . . hell. Now that she'd dropped her disguise, what if those other dudes recognize her?

Oh, well. He'd just have to move fast.

Besides, he told himself with a grin, they might not. If they were like him, they'd paid little attention to her face anyway. He should have enough edge to get first in line.

Upstairs in her room, the debris of her shopping behind her on the bed, Jane was again viewing herself in the mirror.

The face was definitely improved. It should be. She'd been cleansed, pummeled, plucked, and wiped, the red lipstick tsk-tsked, the lashes darkened, the brows shaped, the cheekbones smoothed, and uncounted layers of makeup put over it all.

Yet, improved or not, the face still looked unhappy.

She'd spent far, far too much money. And for what? To look like a tart?

Did she? Did she look like a tart?

She wouldn't if she were thin and wispy. But she was not thin and wispy. "My dear, you are simply opulent," the clerk in the shop had said. And while Jane was dressing, she'd heard her add to the other clerk, "My God—that small waist and those fantastic breasts!" Jane, who had been taught that "those fantastic breasts" were not quite—well—nice, had blushed crimson, and buried her hot face in the dress she was pulling on.

The face wasn't hot now. It hardly felt—or looked—like her face. The phrase "not even her mother would know her" drifted uneasily into Jane's mind. Worse—if she creamed it all off tonight as instructed, would she really be able to put it back on again, the way it looked now?

She had a neat case of cosmetics, shiny and new, that had cost a fortune. And the clerk had said consolingly, "Just think of it as frosting a cake, dear."

Well, thought Jane slowly. *It's done. And inside the frosting I know I'm not a tart.*

But what would other people think?

She glanced at her watch. Nine o'clock and she was starving.

35

Now, with the original paint job still intact, was the time to find out about other people.

Jane took a deep breath, smoothed the soft wine-red velour over her rounded hips, picked up the new clutch bag containing the rather alarmingly depleted wad of money, and headed for the door.

As she dropped her room key inside her purse, her eye was caught by Howard's diamond. Slowly, with a sense of utter depravity, she drew it off and left it on the desk.

The wall by the elevator was mirrored. While she waited, Jane looked at herself again, half pleased and half scared. Dark champagne the hairdresser had called her hair. It curled nicely around her ears and throat.

The elevator doors opened and closed, zipping her down to the lobby, which was deserted. Laughter and chatter was flowing from beyond a grilled door labeled Banquet Room.

At the entrance to the restaurant Jane paused uncertainly. It was almost empty, yet the sign said WAIT TO BE SEATED. Being a polite girl, Jane waited. All the time she was conscious of her toes in slim new pumps, and wished she could smell her own perfume.

An elegant woman with an armload of poster-sized menus sailed up and said, "One? This way, please," in a totally disinterested voice, and conducted her through a bevy of empty tables to a tiny space by swag-draped windows.

"Gorgeous dress," she added in an undertone.

Surprised, Jane said, "Thank you. It's new." The reply was rather ingenuous, but she'd not learned to be otherwise. Not yet.

"Your waitress will be here in a moment," the hostess continued in her previous tone. "Would you like a drink before dinner?"

Jane froze. Then to her rescue swept the mental picture of her mother's favorite TV soap opera—and Liz, the beautiful bitch, saying coolly, "Yes, please. A Chablis—very cold." Or was that a martini? Had she goofed already?

Apparently not. The hostess merely nodded, wrote it down and swept away.

Conscious of having coped with one new experience without stammering and rather pleased with herself, Jane turned her attention to the enormous menu.

Her enthusiasm turned to dismay as she read the prices. Good grief! At home she could eat for a week on the money asked for one lobster dinner. Besides, shells and claws were pretty formidable if you weren't sure how to handle them. Steak and quail, now—that sounded better. Exotic too.

". . . and roquefort dressing," she told the little waitress in the Bavarian lederhosen, almost giggling as she imagined Howard's face. The waitress swept up the menu and trotted off. Pleased with herself again, Jane glanced at the window. She saw nothing there but blackness with a few dim, twinkling lights. Then she turned her attention to the rest of the diners.

I must look detached, cool and amused, she thought, and assumed what she hoped was a detached, cool, and amused expression. This was going to be fun, like the time she'd played Greta and had four whole lines in the junior class play. Greta had been a strumpet, but Jane had concealed that fact from her mother until Mrs. Doorn had read it in the playbill: "Greta, a loose woman with a heart of gold." Mrs. Doorn had almost had a heart attack, but of course it was far too late then to stop Jane. It had been one of the happiest evenings of Jane's life.

Until now.

Under lifted brows, she surveyed the room. Its decor was a sort of Bavarian kitsch, with a lot of wooden wine kegs, plastic bunches of grapes in improbable colors, and a half dozen paintings of the Alps. In one corner sat a family with two exuberant, messy toddlers. An older gentleman was bulwarked by newspapers. A pair of teen-agers, dressed up and self-conscious, sedately ate their salads. Three rigidly coiffed matrons sat beyond Jane, each of them spooning enormous desserts, whipped cream and strawberries. Her empty stomach growled.

A waft of perfume preceded the hostess, who took a stemmed and misting glass filled with pale yellow from her tray and placed it on a tiny napkin before Jane.

37

"Chablis blanc. Compliments," she added softly, "of the gentleman at the bar."

Completely off-guard, Jane turned her head and looked.

She could see part of the lounge through elaborate wooden arches. On a padded stool at the end sat a lanky tanned man in a blazer and turtleneck sweater, his dark hair a shining smooth cap beneath the muted bar lights. He smiled, and raised his own stemmed glass in a silent toast.

Hoping she still wore the cool, detached, and amused look, because her heart was thudding furiously, Jane raised hers back, then turned around again so that she couldn't see him. She was absolutely scared to death.

Was she going to be picked up? That's what men in bars did; she'd watched as much television as anyone. She *knew*.

Desperately she gulped from the glass and came close to gagging. The only wine she'd ever had had been heavy and sweet; this stuff was light, sharp and rather bitter, and she'd swallowed too much at once. Tears came to her eyes but she managed to control them. *Sip, you idiot,* she told herself angrily. *That's the way people drink wine!*

But what about the man in the bar? She couldn't turn and look again. That would be foolish. She thought of the tiny mirror in her bag, got it out, and focused over her shoulder.

The stool was empty!

Her relief, however, was short-lived. The stool was empty because he was now strolling toward her table, followed by the little waitress with two platters.

"I do hope you won't wind," he said affably, bending over her to squash out his cigarette in her ashtray. "I hate eating alone."

All she needed to say was, But I *do* mind! But she'd been taught not to be rude. Besides, he was already folding his long length beneath her table and picking up his napkin so the waitress could place the smoking platter of steak before him. Weakly Jane said, "Thank you for the wine."

"My pleasure."

He had a deep, rather pleasant voice, and very gray eyes that blandly mirrored simple friendliness. Besides, Jane told herself sternly, girls didn't get seduced in public restaurants before an elderly gentleman, two teen-agers, a family of four, and three fat club women. Oh, no! The seduction—and well she knew from ten years of soap operas—the seduction came afterward.

"Tom Nelson," he said. "From St. Croix."

"Crystal Bell," she said, and felt a false surge of security at the pseudonym. It was like a mask she could hide behind.

"Just traveling through?" he asked.

"Yes."

"Me too."

The smell rising from her own platter made her almost faint. She picked up her knife and fork and tried to cut her food without shaking. If he wanted to talk, she resolved, let him do it.

He didn't. The silence became awkward, but she refused stubbornly to break it. They both ate until everything was gone.

Then, leaning back, he patted his lean stomach and sighed comfortably. "Now," he said, and almost seemed to be laughing, "shall we have some more scintillating conversation, or would you like to dance?"

In terror she realized that a disco group had set up in the lounge and was pouring out an organized discord. Stiffly she answered, "I . . . don't dance."

He shrugged. "I suppose not," he answered, "at least, not with amateurs," which to her torpid brain made no sense at all. "All right, your turn. What would you like to do?"

It came out desperately, without her thinking: "Go up to my room."

He blinked, then shrugged again. "Not subtle," he said, "and a bit unexpected. That is—so soon. But, okay. I'd love to. Do you want to finish your wine or take it with us?"

Then she realized what she had said. She gulped. Horrified, she stammered, "No, no, you misunderstood! Please! I meant— by myself. I'm very tired."

He shrugged again.

"I'm the one who's sorry," he said. "But, again, it's okay. Lady's choice. Perhaps I'll see you tomorrow."

He tossed down his napkin, and strolled off to pay his bill. She watched him go, feeling disappointed. She'd wanted an adventure, hadn't she? Why else had she run away?

Unbidden, Howard came to mind. Helplessly she pictured him with the soft, shaven cheeks and the bulge of fat around his middle. She watched Tom Nelson, lean and fit, pulling out bills from his wallet, giving the hostess an engaging grin. His hair looked soft and thick, and his hands were brown and long-fingered.

He took his change, looked back, gave Jane a wry salute, and then went through the lobby out of sight.

She sighed a rather trembly sigh—and sipped her wine. An exciting encounter had been right there. And she'd botched it.

The wine was warm now, and she really didn't want anymore. He'd left a tip. She left one twice the size, paid her own bill, and walked out of the restaurant feeling absurdly young and alone.

But as she pressed the button for her floor, Tom Nelson stepped into the elevator beside her. Instinctively she put out a hand as though to arrest the closing door. He caught it, pulled it back out of harm's way, and dropped it again, all in one motion.

"Look, babe," he said, his voice cold, "if we don't share a bed, we can certainly share an elevator."

She said, "Oh," in a very small voice, and "Good night," equally small, as they both stepped out on the third floor.

He answered, "Yeah," unlocked the door across the hall from hers, and went inside.

She inserted her key in the lock but the door wouldn't open. She tried and tried, almost in a panic.

Tom appeared in the hall once again, an ice bucket in hand. He'd taken off his blazer and shoes. "What's the matter now?" he asked distantly.

"My—my door won't unlock."

He put down the ice bucket, and padded over to help.

"Try putting the key in right side up," he said crossly and opened the door. He started back across the hall.

She took a huge, frightened breath. Her voice came out wavery and uncertain. "I—I've changed my mind. You may come in if you like."

He stopped dead, and wheeled around. The hall light struck pinpoints of ice in his gray eyes and suddenly he seemed eight feet tall.

Then—almost as if someone had pushed a button—he relaxed and smiled. "All right," he said. "After a little. I have some calls to make. Is there a signal to let me in—like three raps and a scratch?"

She swallowed and answered faintly, "No, just knock."

The nervousness that made her voice whispery to her made it sensuous to him. "How about 'Open, sesame'?" he asked.

She missed the point entirely, saying, "All right. I'll—see you later."

"Later," he answered, and was left staring at her closed door. Why did he have a sense of things not going right? It was pretty plain, wasn't it? She was available, after all—and *all* was probably what he was expected to give.

He had a strong feeling that his sister Karen wouldn't approve —but what the hell? If Crystal Bell could be enticed to Limeberry Cove, the people and the money she'd bring with her just might put the season in the black. And how they needed it! If not—well, a roll in the hay was a roll in the hay . . .

Jane leaned against the other side of the door. Her heart was pounding like a piston, and her knees were weak.

She had invited a man to her room! Her bedroom! Which had a bed in it!

Well, what else would a motel room have, you idiot, she asked herself. *That doesn't mean you have to get in it. There are chairs, you know!*

And very comfortable chairs, she added, telling her knees to stiffen and her heart to stop that nonsense. There was also a television to watch. She'd have him call room service for coffee, and they'd chat and watch television and have a pleasant time, and about midnight she'd tell him firmly it was time to go.

Wouldn't she?

On the soap operas they didn't. There was always a close-up

41

of embracing and shut eyes and kissing and violins as the picture faded—so different from Howard's awkward gropings and wet mouth. Surely she wasn't looking for that sort of thing.

Wasn't she?

Of course not, she told herself indignantly and took a deep breath. She was a grown woman. She could handle it.

First she tidied up the room, picking up packages and boxes, and stowing them in the closet. Then she turned on the television, quickly flipping channels until she found a variety show with singing and dancing. That should do nicely. Then she looked at herself.

Well, there was no getting around it. The red dress did show a lot of Jane—especially when she bent forward. But what else should she put on?

The old phrase came to mind: "Get into something comfortable." Sure, Jane. Sure. Put on a nightie, sit on the side of the bed, and have him lay two dollars on the dresser.

Jane found herself blushing.

That's not what I was thinking about, she told herself angrily. But she had just spent eighty-three dollars for an ivory satin nightgown with a matching negligee—a robe, really, that reached the floor, tied around her waist and would reach clear up to her chin. Certainly more clothes than the dress!

She put on the ivory nightgown, looked at herself in the mirror, got very pink, put on the negligee and arranged it so that it reached her chin.

There, she told herself carefully, *I'm as covered as though I had on mother's old flannel housecoat. . . . Although perhaps I shouldn't have taken off my bra. I do kind of—bobble—when I move.*

But, good God, I'm not going to do the tango!

She fluffed her hair and looked at herself again. Despite a small sense of misgiving, she felt an unaccustomed surge of satisfaction.

Mother wouldn't have approved at all. Mother had favored shapeless jumpers over oxford cloth shirtwaists, and heavy brassieres that made Jane look like she had a sofa bolster stuffed down her front. But Mother wasn't here.

The television set was aimed at the bed. Jane turned it more toward a chair, and lugged the other chair around the bed, putting it beside the first one. That wouldn't do. It looked too obvious. She lugged it back. He could sit on the bed and she'd take the chair with the small table between them.

She sat down on the chair, first with her knees crossed, then on one leg. She liked that. It was casual, and she could turn easily toward the bed; besides, she could see herself in the mirror from the corner of her eye and the soft satin folds of her gown fell in a lovely drape when she sat sideways.

There was a knock at the door. With her foot trapped beneath her, Jane almost fell getting up. Her heart was in her mouth. She couldn't do it. She just couldn't do it.

She opened the door and too upset to notice who it was croaked, "Go away."

The elderly gentleman with the bucket of ice blinked and said, "Sorry, I forgot my glasses; I guess I'm next door." Next door an elderly lady called, "In here, Fred. Hello, Mr. Nelson."

Mr. Nelson, who was just coming out his door, answered cheerfully, "Hello, Mrs. Williams, did you get your window open? Here"—he turned to Jane—"grab this before I drop it."

Automatically Jane caught the bottle of wine. He waved two glasses at Mrs. Williams, who said, "Yes, thank you," and closed her door behind her husband. Then Tom calmly preceded Jane into her room. She followed helplessly, her unspoken protest drowned in his cheerful conversation.

"Sorry I took so long," he said. "The telephone system seems to be getting worse instead of better. Have you noticed that? Then I tried to take a shower and I swear everyone else on the floor had the same idea. All I got was a miserable trickle. How's your shower working?"

"Fine. Okay."

"You look delicious."

"Th—thank you."

He had put the two glasses on the table and was easing the

cork from the bottle. It came out with a loud pop. He poured pale foaming yellow into each of the plastic motel glasses, and, in a sort of numb shock, Jane watched him pour. He was swathed from head to heel in a dark velour dressing gown. His hair was damp and gently waving. He smelled of soap and cleanliness, and this time he looked ten feet tall. He grinned at her from this vast height, held out one of the glasses, and said, "Cheers."

"Cheers," she replied, taking a sip. It was good champagne, better than the stuff they'd had at the office Christmas party.

He pulled the belt a little tighter about his waist, sipped his own champagne, and waited for clues. She curled up in the chair. He took the bed, stretching out long legs and arranging his robe decorously. The television was pouring out operatic music as it led into some old movie.

She watched him plump the pillow beneath his head, find it inadequate, take the other, and stuff it behind the first. "Are you comfortable now?" she asked.

He turned and grinned. His robe had loosened, showing a dark mat of hair on his bare brown chest. She tried not to look. "I'm fine for the nonce," he said. "Are you?"

"Quite."

The leg beneath her was going to sleep, but she didn't dare move it. And she was drinking her champagne too fast, but she couldn't seem to help that either. He reached out a long arm and poured another glassful. She drank that too, then glued her eyes desperately to the television screen, watching the moving figures, keenly aware of Tom watching her.

Suddenly he said quietly, "Turn it off."

"What?"

"Turn it off. We don't need it."

Warning bells rang. "But—"

"Television is for people who have nothing better to do."

She tried to stand up, but once more her gown betrayed her— the gown, and the very numb leg inside it. Instead of standing erect, she pitched forward. Wine cascaded down the front of both their robes as with a swift swinging of legs he caught her, laughing. "Whoa!" he exclaimed.

Helpless, she grasped his arms, her one foot a dead weight beneath her. "Oh!" she cried, as the cold wine trickled into vulnerable places. His voice was a rich chuckle in her ear.

"Baby, baby, I'm ready too, but I never thought you'd do a flying act—I almost missed!" The last words were muffled as his mouth slid down the warm column of her throat in little butterfly kisses.

Indignant, her head reeling with the wine, she gasped, "My leg's asleep, you idiot! Stop it! Can't you see I'm wet?"

"Well, then, we'll fix that in a jiffy."

Shifting her to the curve of one arm, he expertly divested her of the negligee, tossed it into an ivory pool on the floor, flipped down the bedcovers, scooped her up with his other arm beneath her knees, and laid her on the cool linen sheet, sitting down beside her. It was all done so swiftly and neatly that she was there before her wine-dazzled brain could comprehend what was going on. All she could manage was a small, muffled, "What are you doing?"

"I'll rub your leg, sweetheart. Benefactor to the world, that's me—never thinking of myself. Which one is it—this one or this one?"

His hard, warm hand slid up beneath the rumpled satin, stroking first one round thigh, then the other. The impish grin on his face suddenly changed to something less impish. She gasped like a fish, pulling both legs beneath her, struggling upright. The world, whirling before her, mirrored only one image—his brown, broad, velour-framed chest, coming closer. She thrust out both hands; they found no purchase on hard, muscular ribs, only slid around to his back. Her mouth, trying to say something in dizzy protest, said nothing as his own found hers, taking complete and savage possession. Suddenly she was clinging in simple, mindless limbo, and in her singing ears she heard his deep voice say softly, "That's better. That's my girl." His mouth slid to her throat in subtle caresses. One hand slipped the thin strap of her nightgown down her shoulder, stroking the satin skin. Of her own betraying, instinctive volition, one of her hands went up the strong column of his neck, her fingers seeking his soft, thick dark hair. A sort of ripple went through his body; she felt it tense against her own. Then his gentle, searching hand went downward over the opulent curves of her bare breasts.

That was when the long, sharp sword of her mother's teaching reached from the grave and pierced through to reality.

It was like an electric shock—a cold, ugly bolt of lightning. She stiffened, tore loose, and rolled away from him. When in total incomprehension he followed, she slapped his face savagely, and cried out, "Get away! Get away! I hate you!"

A desperate, hunted animal, she burrowed beneath the bed-covers and huddled, shaking, panting, fearful.

After a long moment she felt him get up. She couldn't see him staring downward, puzzled, angry, struggling between arousal and stupefaction.

"What the hell is the matter with you?" he said through clenched teeth.

Nothing in the magazines had said this broad was kinky—and her first reaction had been pure, straight female desire. He was certainly no novice. He hadn't misread the signals—what she'd given had been simple and direct. But politics or not, he'd never been one to go where he wasn't wanted.

His jaw set angrily, he re-tied the belt of his robe with cold, sharp tugs, and said in a hard voice, "Good night, Miss Bell!" He stalked out of the room.

She heard the door slam. It was like a blow against her heart.

She began to cry—first a whimper, lost and lonely, then great wrenching sobs, full of misunderstanding and self-pity. And inside her rumpled head another Jane was crying too, crying for the glimpse of something Howard Van Tassel had never been able to give, had no capacity to give.

After a long time she got up wearily, locked the door, stripped off the satin nightgown, and took as cold a shower as she could bear. Then, not looking at herself, she got into the old flannel gown and huddled back into bed. It was a long time before she slept.

CHAPTER IV

She'd never spent as desolate a night in her life. Even her mother's death—the sense of loss she'd faced then—had not been like this. Mother had prepared her, had handed her over to Howard and died content—not realizing that her beloved child was merely going from one form of bondage to another.

Jane had sensed it then. She knew it now.

But she was still not prepared to break the bonds. Howard meant security, a place in the proper scheme of things—everything the people in her hometown seemed to place in importance above all else. If she humiliated Howard, he was lost to her forever. She couldn't risk that.

Yet what a child she had truly been! She had wanted an adventure, a little romance before entering Howard's box forever imagining that such things would leave her untouched, uninvolved—that an adventure would be as simple as going to a movie, as easy to shake off when the movie was over. What a child she had been! What an *idiot!*

Mother had been right. There were men with strong arms and soft black hair who were—what was it Mother always said—just out for a good time. She'd found one. What she hadn't known was that *she* was vulnerable.

And she was. She was very vulnerable. . . .

She had contributed her bit. She must be honest. A new dress, a new face, and too much wine. And she'd thought she was Sophia Loren.

Well, she wasn't. Far from it. Mother's child had got in beyond her depth and the waters had almost swallowed her.

Inept, amateur, naive—she called herself all those bitter names, adding to them the subtle sting that somehow in her confused dismay she'd also perhaps been unfair.

She wept mournfully into her pillow, and her wet cheeks were crimson with shame. *Will I have to see him again? What will I say?*

Or will he avoid me?

Muddled, her mind battered with indecision, she finally drifted off to sleep, a soggy wad of Kleenex in one hand and her hair straying across the blurry remains of Elizabeth Arden's best. Then she dreamed that Mother Van Tassel had taken her new negligee, was trying to fasten it over her corset and bulges, that she herself in nothing but the satin nightgown, was running over cold, wet snow, that Howard said, "My darling, wait, I'll keep you warm," and his arms were holding her. . . .

But the arms were long, not short, and the hands were not pudgy and groping, but strong and knowing. His stringy, thin hair had turned soft and thick, his pink cheeks hard. She melted, murmuring out loud with the joy of melting.

She woke up.

Stiff with disillusion, she stared around at the disheveled bed, the gray light from closed curtains slanting across the ivory puddle that was the negligee on the floor.

Then she remembered last night. What should she do? Quit? Slink home like a whipped pup?

No!

She'd call that travel agency, find that island with its promises of white sand and warm sun, leave behind this dirtied place of defeat and humiliation.

She slid her feet to the floor, put on the satin robe, went into the bathroom and began to remove what was left of yesterday's makeup. The ragged Kleenex matched her mood, especially when she was done and in the mirror saw good old muddy-colored Jane again.

The two Janes regarded each other. One of them suddenly but distinctly said an extraordinarily dirty word.

She'd heard it from Sally, deplored it, never imagined she herself would ever be so coarse. But today that word was exactly right . . . so right, in fact, that she said it again.

She was *not* going to let herself be beaten!

She'd just spent a lot of money to improve herself, and she

meant to use the improvements. If later Howard didn't like her new face, she'd decide then whether to revert to her old self or not; but today she was certainly not going to go around looking like the unburied dead.

She undressed, took a quick shower, put on some of the incredibly brief and filmy bits of underclothes, and padded back to the mirror over the sink.

She decided to tone down the makeup. The spidery lashes stayed in their little box along with the eye shadow. The blush went on a bit lopsided; she had to cream it off and start over. The second time was better. She had her lips outlined when she realized she hadn't scrubbed her teeth.

In the middle of brushing her teeth it struck her—and she stopped, transfixed, toothpaste dribbling down her chin. Never before in her entire life had she stood before a mirror practically naked! Her mother hadn't approved of the human body. She'd even tried to get her daughter a doctor's excuse from gym so she wouldn't have to take communal showers.

Mouth still full of paste, she turned sideways and sucked in her stomach. She was a little—Junoesque—but not bad.

Suddenly she remembered the subtle, searching slide of Tom Nelson's hands—and resumed scrubbing her teeth in a hurry, bent over the sink. That kind of thinking would bring nothing but defeat, and this morning she needed all the positive thoughts she could garner.

With a nail clipper she snipped the price tags from a toast-colored pair of slacks and matching sweater, pulled them on, and admired her tousle-headed image in the mirror. Then she sat on the bed, one foot curled beneath her, scrabbled in her old bag for the ad for the travel agency, took a deep breath, and dialed.

A deep pleasant voice said, "Limeberry Cove Vacations. May I help you?"

Cut it out! Jane said angrily to her jumping heart. *I suppose every male voice now is going to sound like Tom Nelson's!*

Her voice was undeniably croaky as she answered. "Yes, please." She cleared her throat twice. "Excuse me. I—I—I saw your ad in our paper—about three days at your resort for $500."

"Yes, ma'am. Three days, four nights, and everything paid but gratuities. The sunshine is free." *And Karen is going to lose her socks on this one unless I can pull it off,* Tom Nelson said grimly to himself, doodling dying palm trees on a scratch pad. The chick on the other end of the line sounded like another loser—some bumpy-faced secretary with a few bucks saved in a Christmas Club. *And I had to be a real smartass and muck it up with Crystal Bell!* he thought.

Jane swallowed again. "Tell me when I would go, please, and what I have to do."

"Very good!" Tom replied, putting charm into his voice. "There's a flight out at one o'clock tomorrow. Our Miss Turner will meet you at the Air Illinois desk in the Quincy terminal and put you on the feeder flight to St. Louis. Our charter leaves half an hour later with one brief stop in Miami. You'll be at Limeberry Cove in time for dinner."

Tomorrow! Jane gave a small, unbelieving gasp. "How about the—the payment?" she said faintly.

"Miss Turner will have your tickets at the airport. You can pay her then. Just give me your name, and the number of people in your party."

"Oh, of course. My name is—" And there was the faintest hesitation; then she continued firmly. "—Jane Doorn. D-O-O-R-N. And there's just me. One in the party, I mean."

"Fine. Welcome to Limeberry Vacations, Miss Doorn. You're allowed forty pounds of luggage, but remember—the only winter clothes you'll need will be for St. Louis. The sun is shining in St. Croix."

St. Croix. Why did that remind her of Sioux City?

His pleasant, resonant voice went on. "Are there any other questions?"

"No—not that I think of."

He heard the perplexity in her tone. "Well, if there are, please feel free to call us at this number. We want you to have a happy trip."

"Thank you."

"Good morning, then."

50

"Good morning."

She hung up, glanced around, got up, and tugged open the drapes. Soft snow was wetly smacking the glass. Seeing it, Jane giggled. The sun was shining in St. Croix!

And tomorrow—tomorrow at one o'clock—she'd be going there!

What did she need to do now? She hoped the clothes she'd bought yesterday would be all right because she certainly couldn't afford to buy more. But that suitcase! Good grief. It must weigh forty pounds by itself. Something lightweight, soft-sided, and cheap.

Back to the mall. That would be the best place to go. She remembered a little coffee shop there; she'd have some breakfast later.

Actually humming, she cleaned up the mess in the bathroom, hanging the towels neatly so they would dry. Then she folded her clothes and made the bed. There. Now she could go.

As she locked her own door, she noted that the one door to Tom Nelson's room was open. Her heart caught until she realized that the place was empty, the bedsheets crumpled untidily, and the spread piled on the floor.

A maid was trundling a cleaning cart down the hall. Jerking her head at Tom's room, Jane said disdainfully, "I guess some people enjoy living like pigs."

"Yes, ma'am," the maid replied. One shouldn't question the guests, the maid admitted, but to her Mr. Nelson was one of the better kind; she'd been sorry to notice him checking out that morning.

A whining wind slapped Jane in the face as she went outside to her car. She started the engine, turned the wipers on to clear off the snow, then with collar huddled around her ears, she slid back out to mop at the rear windows with a napkin. Shivering, she got inside again. The wipers had given her two clean fans to see through, and the view was dandy—a dirty stack of last week's snow, over which the new stuff was blowing in from the river in wet spikes.

Tomorrow, she said to herself. *Tomorrow I'll be out of all of this!*

The streets were just a touch slick, and since her car seemed to want to die at each intersection, the trip back out to the mall was not enjoyable. Jane scurried into the nearest entrance, aided by the wind trying to use her coat as a sail, then stood a moment in the welcome heat, loosening her collar, shaking her head free of snow, and trying to get her breath back.

On her right by the entrance to the Sears store was the theater lobby with enormous posters of a disaster movie flanked by other posters of Disney characters. To her left stretched a long corridor of stores. Then, farther down, her roving eye was caught by a brace of travel agencies flaunting their cruise ships and marimba bands in large glossies. Quickly her new shoes took her in that direction. She found Limeberry Vacations, although it was not quite as flamboyant as the others and a great deal smaller.

There was a gray-haired lady at the counter; she smiled and asked, "May I help you?"

Jane started. She had unconsciously been looking for the owner of the deep, pleasant voice she'd heard on the phone. Hastily she gathered her scattered wits. Should she say she'd already been helped? Should she say she was going on one of their vacations tomorrow?

She was seized with sudden timidity. She stuttered something trite about the awful weather. The lady nodded.

"I know. Isn't it nice to realize there are places that aren't all cold and snow. Here, dear, take a few of our brochures; perhaps they'll make you feel warmer."

"Oh, thank you. Thank you very much."

"That's our guest house," the lady said, pointing with a pencil tip. "You can lie in bed and hear the ocean. It sort of whispers across the sand. This is Mrs. Sutton—she owns Limeberry—she and her brother. In fact he's leaving this morning for St. Louis to take a group over tomorrow. You just missed him. They're such nice people to work for, I do hope—oh. Excuse me. The telephone."

Jane moved on, nodding her thanks and stuffing the brochures in her bag to read later—to savor this evening while the wind whimpered around the corners of the motel. What she really needed at the moment was a luggage shop and some coffee.

Finding the luggage shop was easy but finding an acceptable price was not. What did they make those things of—unicorn hide? However, that fawn-colored overnighter with the matching dressing case was so pretty and just what she needed.

Carrying the fawn-colored overnighter and the matching dressing case, her funds sadly depleted, Jane looked around for a coffee shop.

There was a cafeteria just across the cobblestone area, and she got in line, shifting her awkward burden so that she could slide her tray along. The gentleman in front of her was wearing a fawn-colored suit—in fact it almost matched her luggage. Bemused by this, Jane selected a cup of coffee, a glass of water, and a large Danish with melted butter pooled on its top.

The cashier, on her tall stool, was saying to the gentleman, "A dollar fifty, sir," and he was reaching into his hip pocket. Jane was juggling the dressing case and tray to get to her own money, when the man behind her suddenly shoved forward.

Jane cried "Oh!" in horror, as the corner of her tray tipped. The coffee, the water, and the Danish all slid right onto those lovely fawn-colored pants and down one leg.

The coffee was hot. The gentleman yelled, and Jane found herself staring upward into the outraged eyes of Tom Nelson.

Tears brimming instantly, she gulped, "Oh, I'm sorry—I'm so sorry—"

"You're sorry! I'm the one who has to catch a plane in twenty minutes wearing pants that look like I cooked breakfast on them!"

"Let me get them cleaned . . . I'll buy you new ones. . . . I'll—"

"Oh, cram it," he said angrily, sopping at the mess with a busboy's rag. "I know you're sorry. I understand. Quit bawling and go drink your coffee. Mabel, get her another cup."

Tut-tutting, Mabel hopped off her stool and obeyed.

"But—" Jane said piteously.

"It's all right," he said "I *forgive* you. Good-bye."

His long, spotted legs took him across the cobblestones. Through blurred eyes she saw him pick up a suitcase and vanish inside a door marked MEN. The cashier said sympathetically, "Here, hon. Don't worry. He's all right."

Suddenly realizing that not only had she made an idiot of herself but she was also holding up the entire line, Jane gulped, snuffled, took the coffee very carefully, and moved to an obscure table. But the coffee was like dishwater in her mouth.

A few minutes later she saw Tom Nelson come out again dressed in a different pair of slacks, the wet ones over his arm. Without looking to see if she was still there he walked off out of sight down the mall.

Feeling even more desolated, Jane gathered her purchases and went back out of the warm shopping center into the blowing cold.

Her car was covered with a light frosting of snow and filled with a raw dampness. It started with some reluctance, gray smoke pouring from the exhaust. Jane turned on the heater and defrosters full force. The engine started to die. Grimly she kept a heavy foot on the accelerator. In the opaque half light of the snow-covered windows, she laid her head on her arms against the steering wheel.

She was not going to cry. Yes, she was. She wept quiet, wet, gulping sobs, pounding the wheel rim with a closed fist.

She was pawing blindly in her bag for more Kleenex when the Buick engine—whining and coughing, its warning unheeded— suddenly burst forth into a full-throated, shattering protest. Something seemed to explode, banging against the underside of the hood. The entire car lurched forward, shuddered, then fell into ominous silence. A thin wisp of smoke rolled away into the gray air.

Frightened out of her wits, Jane scrambled out of the car to safety against the hood of a nearby Ford. A gentleman in a small Pinto three cars down slid out from his own front seat, scuffled through the snow to the Buick, and touched the warm hood

54

gently. Then he reached inside, pulled the hood release and raised it. He looked at the interior, and whistled.

"Lady," he said to the wild-eyed girl against the Ford, "you may as well call a tow car. You have a severe problem."

Just how severe Jane didn't realize until the wrecker man, in stocking cap and shoe pacs, licked a bare thumb and flipped the papers on his clipboard.

"I can't really say," he told the miserable girl standing apprehensively beside him. "The rod went through the block. She's pretty scrambled. But—at a guess—six hundred dollars will do it. And four—maybe five—days. Depending on parts." He had already sized up the leather coat and the neat shoes; she was probably good for it. "Shall I haul her away?"

What choice did she have?

Almost numb with despair, Jane nodded. There went the vacation. There went everything.

"What's your name, miss?"

"Jane Doorne. I'm—I'm staying at the motel down the road."

"I'll have to ask for a retainer," he said.

She merely nodded, and opened her bag. "How much?"

"A hundred bucks."

She paid it in twenties, and he saw more where they came from. Reassured, he softened somewhat. "Listen. You're stuck, aren't you? My place is just up the street. If you don't mind riding in the wrecker, we'll put the car in the shop, then someone can run you over to your motel."

Twenty minutes later a rather greasy gentleman in an ancient Volkswagen deposited Jane at the portals of the motel with a cheery, "Y'all keep in touch, now!"

"Yeah," said Jane grimly.

She stood still for a moment, holding her brand new luggage—which she didn't need now. Behind her the Volkswagen chugged away through the slush, and she didn't know it was gone.

Six hundred dollars.

She only had six hundred and fifty left. Not only was the vacation down the tube. She could not live at the motel five more days on fifty dollars.

Oh, she had her checkbook.

No, she didn't. Howard had taken it on Monday to balance, as he always did.

And no credit cards. She, Sally, and another girl at work had applied for one once, but Howard had sent hers back. When they were married, he'd said, his cards would do for both of them.

The knowledge of what she must do now almost made her ill. She had to call Howard, and let him make some sort of financial arrangement for her.

She'd almost rather die. . . .

"Damn!" Cold, shivering, and very scared, she picked up her new luggage and went up the icy steps into the warm motel lobby.

The lovely smells of coffee and lunch floated out on the limpid air from the Bavarian dining room as she plodded by. She ignored them. The elevator was empty. So was the hallway.

She struggled briefly with the room key, went inside, slammed the door shut, and dumped her luggage onto the bed. The telephone on the table next to it loomed large.

All the way up in the elevator she'd been doing frantic addition in her head and it all had come out the same: zero. She thought of how everyone laughed hilariously at people doing stacks of dishes because they couldn't pay their bills in the movies. But what *did* they do when you couldn't pay? In real life did you get arrested?

The awful vision of Howard coming to bail her out was worse than making a phone call first. Kicking off her wet shoes, burying her cold toes in the warm shag rug, Jane took a deep breath, gritted her teeth, and dialed.

It was Thursday and after twelve, which meant the bank was closed. Howard lunched at home. On the first Thursday of the month he took his mother to the cemetery with a floral offering for his father's grave. On the other three they either turned mattresses or stuck green stamps in little books—whichever chore was more pressing.

The phone rang twice before Mrs. Van Tassel answered in her best society matron's voice.

56

"I'm sorry," she said. "He is at the bank. He has a very important meeting with some out-of-town financiers." Then her tone sharpened. "Janet! Janet, is that you?"

Jane, however, was long gone. She was already dialing another familiar number.

It rang and rang. When she'd almost given up, the receiver was lifted, and on a faint waft of Waylon Jennings singing "Luckenbach Texas" a giggly voice said, "Duffy's Tavern, Duffy ain't here."

Incredulously, Jane said, "Sally?"

Click! The line went dead.

Jane stared at the receiver in her hand, then at the round, numbered disk that had betrayed her.

She must have dialed work instead of the bank. Sally better not let Mr. Elbert, Jane's boss, catch her answering the phone like that!

But Thursday was Sally's afternoon off! Could she have rung Sally's apartment?

This time she dialed painstakingly, making certain each digit added up to the bank's correct number.

Howard answered, sounding annoyed. Of course he was annoyed. He didn't like to be interrupted when he was doing business.

"Howard—" she said, and he cut right across her.

"Jane, where are you? What's going on?"

"My—my car has had an accident."

"Damn. I knew something would happen. How much is it going to cost?"

Not "Were you hurt?" Just "How much is it going to cost?"

Reluctantly Jane mumbled, "Six—six hundred dollars."

"Six hundred dollars! Highway robbery! Well, at least you have the money with you. Or is there any left?"

The unfairness of it hit her like cold water. She gasped. She opened her mouth to protest, but she never said the words, because right then music suddenly blasted into her ear. But not just any music. "Luckenbach Texas" and Waylon and Willie and the boys.

Sally!

Sally plus Howard plus the bank after closing. Howard was having a meeting all right, but finances didn't enter into it—unless it was the fee for a two-dollar broad!

Jane told Howard something she'd brought back from day camp one year as a six-year-old. Her mother had washed out her mouth with soap. She said it as clearly as though she'd been practicing it ever since. Then she hung up. Bang!

But after about thirty seconds the bubble of outrage burst against the hard, cold edge of reality, and she was left staring at the dead telephone.

Now what was she going to do?

CHAPTER V

She had just cut off her lifeline, her sole means of financial aid, her only recourse in time of trouble.

It didn't alter her ambivalent outrage. *Of all the perfidious sneaks,* she thought grimly. *What in the world do I do now? Sink or swim, I'll have to do it on my own.*

She got up and trailed forlornly to the window. The snow had stopped; it plastered the shrubbery and burdened the trees. Below her the Mississippi River rolled south, its cold gray waters wind-rowed into foamy whitecaps, its shores bordered with dirty crusts of ice. A large bird flapped slowly by. On the old bridge the cars crawled, smeared with slush and spewing spumes of exhaust on the dank, raw air.

Tears blurred the river, and she mopped at them angrily, thinking: *Good grief, can't I do anything else but cry? There has to be something. . . .*

She had gotten into the habit of twisting her ring when she was upset. The ring wasn't there. She walked over to the bureau, picked it up, then looked at it almost numbly, remembering her disappointment, remembering Howard's explaining how it was just a token. The real Van Tassel family engagement ring was two carats and handsome—only Mother was still wearing it, and it gave her such pleasure he knew Jane wouldn't mind waiting . . .

Slowly she put on this token ring. Slowly she took it off again. Could she pawn it?

Common sense told her probably not. The gold was undoubtedly minimal, the diamond certainly so. Besides, her only knowledge of pawn shops came through having read some lurid novels, and her soul shrank timidly at the idea of trying to pawn it.

She went to her old bag, and dug around for something to drop the ring into. An envelope would do nicely, and she drew out the one from McIlhenny and McIlhenny, her mother's life insurance company.

Suddenly she froze, and her heart seemed to skip a beat. There was supposed to be a check in that envelope. Howard would have a fit—but it was made out to her. Even if it was only for a few hundred dollars she would be saved!

With trembling fingers she tore off one end of the envelope, shut her eyes, murmured a prayer, and drew out the check. She opened her eyes and looked.

Ten thousand dollars!

She knew her mother had been sick a long time—but ten thousand dollars?

Then a mantle of despair settled over her. It may as well be ten million. Where in this city was she, a stranger with no visible credit rating, going to cash a check like that? Particularly, she realized dismally, a stranger registered at the motel under a false name.

"Oh, damn," she said softly through gritted teeth. It was like glimpsing paradise through prison bars. "Damn, damn, damn. What can I do?"

She sank down on the side of the bed, staring at the slip of paper in her cold hands.

She had to find a bank. That was the only place. The chances were slim, but she had to try.

Grimly she rose, looked in the mirror, and grimaced. Tears do not improve the best of faces, and she'd never been able to cry without coming out all mottled red and puffy. She got a face cloth, wrung it out in cold water, lay on the bed, and put it across her eyes for a few minutes while the fears and anxieties rattled against each other in her mind. The silence was oppressive.

She got back up, brushed her hair, buttoned the coat she'd never taken off, picked up her bag and key, and left.

The same enameled blonde was at the desk, smiling the same plastic smile, and it half amused Jane that she showed no signs of recognition. "May I help you?" the woman asked.

"I need to cash a check."

"Of course. If you'll just show us two credit cards and your

60

American Express, I'm sure we can arrange something—"

"I think not," intervened Jane calmly, feeling a perverted pleasure in denying this exotic creature the knowledge that she was one of those extraordinary people without credit cards. "It's for ten thousand dollars."

"Oh." For one moment there was a crack in the enamel. "Oh, dear. You're right. Perhaps a bank . . ."

"Where is one, please?"

"Just up the street and right two blocks. It's a very good bank. We do all our business there."

Jane turned toward the door. The woman called after her, "Miss. Oh, miss!"

Jane stopped and looked back.

The mention of ten thousand dollars had noticeably increased the wattage on the clerk's smile. "Would you like a courtesy car? It's awfully nasty outside."

"That would be nice."

"Just a moment, please. I'll have one sent around."

The wait was somewhat longer than a moment, but Jane didn't quibble. Leaving the driver in the parking lot, she swept regally through the marble portals of the bank. But at the sight of the long row of teller cages and the opulent chairs no one ever sat in, the vaulted ceiling and the soft, piped-in music, her confidence fled. Banks always affected her that way, even Howard's. She felt so inconsequential.

But, she thought, gritting her teeth, *I have ten thousand dollars! Even banks don't sneer at that!*

On a small surge of false courage she stepped up to a vacant window.

The teller wore a three-piece suit and an artfully contrived hairpiece. "Yes, miss," he said briskly.

"I need to cash a check."

"Have you an account here?"

"I'm from out of town."

"Well, we'll see what we can arrange. How much did you want?"

"Ten thousand dollars."

He blinked. "Well," he said. "Yes, I see." As she placed the check before him, he stepped back a bit as though it might explode. "Perhaps we'd better see Mr. Parsons."

He went first. There was a rather long consultation. A gray head popped up briefly over a partition. Mr. Parson, no doubt, casing the strange female with the ten-thousand-dollar check. Then the teller beckoned, and Jane found herself inside the thick-carpeted cubicle.

"Mr. Parson, Miss . . . Doorn," said the teller, and made his exit quickly as though very glad to be rid of the entire situation.

"Ah, Miss Doorn," said Mr. Parsons, who was indeed the gray head, and now firmly ensconced behind his shining mahogany desk. "Please sit down."

He had the check before him. Jane sat down primly on the edge of the leather chair. Then, doggedly refusing to be intimidated, she slid farther back, crossing her legs and smiling what she hoped was a cool smile.

He rested the fingertips of one hand neatly against those of the other and cleared his throat. "Of course you understand this is quite a bit of money."

Jane made a gesture with her head, not trusting her voice.

"We require verification—driver's license, credit cards—some other things. I'm sure you understand."

He seemed strangely tense. *Good grief,* thought Jane, *he probably has one foot on the alarm button. I have ten thousand dollars, and they're treating me as if I stole it!*

The entire day had not been good, and this was the worst of all. Enough was enough. She straightened up in the chair, and to her amazement she heard Mrs. Elbert's voice coming out of her mouth. Mrs. Elbert was master of the I-know-who-I-am-but-who-do-you-think-you-are? technique.

"My dear sir," she said coldly, "let me offer a suggestion. My fiancé is Mr. Howard Van Tassel of the First Holland National Bank. I propose that, one, you check on Mr. Van Tassel's rating with your bankers' association—a rating that, I assure you, is

62

impeccable. Two, you get Mr. Van Tassel himself on the phone and we'll both speak to him."

"Oh," said Mr. Parsons, startled. "Well, perhaps that won't be necessary."

"I insist," said Jane. "Try the bank first, then his home. Take this," she added, sliding Howard's card across the desk. "His residential number is unlisted."

Mr. Parsons frowned, and tapped the desk with his pencil. Then he abruptly scooped up the card and disappeared.

Good grief, Jane thought, *this whole bank is full of jack-in-the-boxes!*

Aware that she might be under surveillance, she struggled to keep the snobbish look on her face, although her heart was jumping like a scared rabbit's. Her real impulse was to grab the check and run—except, she realized in dismay, Mr. Parsons had taken it with him.

She had gambled. Now the whole thing hung on Howard answering the phone and, worse, what he might say.

Why had she ever mentioned Howard? she mourned. Why hadn't she just walked out and thought of another solution?

What was taking them so long? The taped music stopped and started again. This was awful. . . .

Suddenly Mr. Parsons popped back into the cubicle.

"If you would pick up the phone," he said, "and punch button two."

He sat back down and pressed his fingers together again. His face was expressionless.

Jane leaned forward and punched two. Howard's voice said, unbelieving, "Jane?"

Well, they *had* got him. She wondered if he was still at the bank. The memory of her last talk with him helped to keep her voice cool. "Yes, Howard."

"What is all this nonsense about a ten-thousand-dollar check and your being in Quincy, Illinois?"

"It's the McIlhenny check."

"Oh," he answered, and though she was too upset to notice, his voice suddenly took on quite a different tone.

"I told you my car had had an accident, Howard," she went on.

"But, Jane, dear—" Now he spoke in his best banker's manner, one she was all too familiar with—"Surely you don't need ten thousand dollars."

"I need more than I'm carrying. And you have my checkbook."

"So I do. How unfortunate." He was really laying on the sane and reasonable banker bit. *Someone else,* she thought, *must be on an extension here, and Howard knows it.* "Well, dear," he continued, "I'm sure we can work something out. Put me back to Mr. Parsons for a moment, and we'll arrange for a transfer of funds. How much do you need?"

"Two thousand dollars," said Jane, and almost fainted at the sound of her own voice. There was such a long pause she began to wonder if Howard had fainted. But he was back on the line, clearing his throat and struggling against his emotions.

"Well," he said, and the words sounded strangled, "I suppose it can be done. Just put the McIlhenny check away safely, Jane. Let me see—it's one thirty now. I can't possibly arrive in Quincy until five thirty or six, so you will be ready, won't you? I need to be back here in time to pick Mother up at Aunt Lucy's."

"I'm not ready to come home yet, Howard," Jane said.

"Jane, what are you talking about?"

He did sound upset! *Good,* thought Jane. Briskly, she added, "I'll keep in touch. Good-bye, Howard." She handed the telephone back to Mr. Parsons.

Twenty minutes later she was walking back to the motel car, heady with success and two thousand dollars richer—or poorer, as the case might be, as the money had still come from her account. Howard wasn't *that* generous. Also, she was gratified to have had Mr. Parsons personally escort her to the door, making inane little remarks about the terrible weather and how happy they were to have served her. The McIlhenny check was back in her bag again—safe, as Howard had said.

She could mail it to him. Then, perversely, she decided not to.

64

She'd be back home inside a week, and certainly her mother's doctors weren't going to sue Howard Van Tassel's fiancée.

There are advantages, she realized ruefully, as she was driven through the gray, slushy streets back to the motel.

I just hope that there are enough of them.

CHAPTER VI

All the way back to the motel Jane kept saying silently to herself, *Two thousand dollars!*

She could hardly believe it. Of course she would not spend nearly that—but the wonder was Howard's giving in with hardly a murmur. And why? It was very unlike Howard. He couldn't be conscience-stricken. By now he'd probably rationalized his affair with Sally into a story so plausible that he believed it himself.

More likely, having discovered where she was, he planned on taking her home before she could spend it.

Jane smiled wryly at that, because it had the ring of truth. Yet she was amazed at herself. Where had she gotten the courage to say no?

She was undoubtedly piling up trouble on the home front, but just now all she could feel was excitement. She went back into her motel room with renewed pleasure in the bright curtains, the pleasant glow of light through the green glass lamp, the broad, gray river flowing outside her window. Her new luggage was, again, exactly what she needed. *I'll pack tonight,* she promised herself, then was unable to wait. It was such fun to fold the new shorts and tops, the slacks, the one light jacket with its matching shirt, the blue swimsuit and beach robe, and that last lovely extravagance, the thin silk dinner dress, white as a cloud, soft as satin, and made to flow from waist to feet in graceful lines that rippled as she walked. She had to stop and try it on again; it was the most beautiful dress she'd ever owned.

The salesclerk had been right, she thought, eyeing herself critically in the mirror. It did fit much better without a bra. But—would she ever have the nerve?

Probably not, she realized, slipping the dress off.

She left her nightie out, the cranberry dress to wear tomorrow, and the rose-colored one to wear down to dinner. Then she curled up by the lamp with a lap full of Limeberry Cove brochures and—not surprisingly—in a lovely welter of bougainvillaea, white sandy beaches, and windmills, she went to sleep.

She awoke abruptly and absolutely starved—which was not surprising, either, since she'd not eaten all day. It was almost six thirty. After scrubbing her teeth and brushing her hair, she zipped herself into the red dress, and, hungry or not, took time to put perfume in all the proper places.

Then, locking her door, and with her heart beating undeniably fast, she took the elevator down to dinner.

Thomas Nelson was not in the dining room, or, as far as she could see, in the lounge.

Then the words came back to her: "I'm the one who has to catch a plane—"

Of course he wouldn't be in the lounge or anywhere else. He was gone. She'd never see him again. . . .

Unreasonably depressed, she ordered coffee—certainly not wine again—and, sipping it, scanned the menu. Pork chops. Chicken. She could have those at home.

She settled for the mundane—a medium well done steak, baked potato, and salad. With almost unconscious defiance, she also ordered bleu cheese dressing on her salad.

A man in a turtleneck sweater slid onto the end bar stool and her heart shot into her mouth. But he was stocky and bald with thick glasses.

You imbecile, she scolded herself, cutting her steak. *Stop doing that! He's gone. Forget it. Forget it all. Chalk what you can up to experience.*

Saying was simpler than doing. Deeply disturbed by her ambivalent feelings, Jane ate a lonely meal. Everyone else seemed intent on their own affairs. The old gentleman behind her exchanged evening papers with the old gentleman in front of her. The two ladies at the next table compared their digestive processes with a sort of fierce competition. The small child in the high chair made an earnest effort to deposit all his brussels sprouts on the carpet which—Jane thought, as she gathered up her bag—was where brussels sprouts ought to be.

Then, having finished her meal and heading toward the elevator, she had all the excitement she could handle.

She heard the voice first—a familiar voice, raised indignantly. She'd read a lot of novels about a voice "curdling the blood" but she'd never known what it meant. Until then.

The voice was saying, "My dear young woman, I demand to see the register!"

"Sir, I can't let you do that," said the clerk, "but I can assure you that no one of that name is registered among our guests."

"The name is Doorn. D-O-O-R-N. She must be here because she is nowhere else."

Howard!

Jane didn't dare look. She put one foot before the other in a numb line toward the blessed, open doors of the elevator.

A voice transfixed her. The desk clerk's, saying brightly, "Good evening, Miss Bell. I hope you enjoyed your dinner."

"Yes. Yes, thank you," Jane murmured, expecting the hand of doom on her shoulder.

But it didn't happen. Howard gave her only a cursory glance, if he glanced at all. He was saying with deadly patience, "The young woman I am looking for is medium height, with brownish hair and a brownish coat."

"Sir, I can call the manager."

"Please do."

Jane was in the elevator. She was safe.

No, she wasn't.

One of the elderly gentlemen from the dining room came hurrying out. He called, "Hold it for me, will you, miss?"

With a sick feeling she reached out and held the door. She was pushing herself as far into the corner as she could; nonetheless, Howard turned and looked straight at her. She was caught.

She looked straight back, too frozen to smile. His eyes dropped to the red dress, the legs, the shoes. Then he turned to the desk again.

"Good evening, sir," he said. "I am Howard Van Tassel. I'm looking for—"

The door slid mercifully shut on his tale of the girl with the brownish eyes and the brownish coat. The elevator shot upward.

Jane leaned against the wall limply, realizing the incredible. He hadn't recognized her!

Or had he? Was he just playing cat-and-mouse? No, Howard wouldn't do that. She was safe.

But *was* she? Suppose he'd already found the garage? What if he began to put facts together. . . .

The elevator stopped, and the door opened. She scuttled to her door like a small mouse to its hole, tried to put the key in the lock the wrong way, turned it, turned it too far. Moaning under her breath, she turned it again. The door opened. She flew inside, closed and locked the door, ran to the window, and dragged the drapes shut, ignoring the fact there was nothing beyond but the Mississippi River. Then, like a child, she dived for the bed and burrowed beneath the covers, her hands over her ears, not wanting to listen but hardly daring not to.

This was terrible. Howard was treating her like a common runaway—and, in all fairness, she was responding like one.

Why had she bolted? Why hadn't she had the courage to walk up, say, Howard, here I am, I'm sorry you've made the trip, but I'm not going home yet. Why couldn't she have done that? He might have blustered or chided or used the old guilt trick—but she was over twenty-one. He couldn't have carried her off bodily!

Now all she could do was cower in her room and wait for a knock on the door.

No, that wasn't all. Numbly she accepted what she must do.

Slowly she got back up, turned on the light, brushed her hair, smiling grimly as she remembered that Howard had not recognized her, and went back down in the elevator.

She was twenty-two years old. She'd done nothing wrong, and she'd promised to marry this man. Howard was stuffy, spoiled, and dominating, but she'd known that when she'd made the commitment. If they really couldn't be honest with each other, she'd better find it out right now.

The elevator door slid open. She took a deep, shaky breath and stepped out.

Howard was gone!

She actually felt disappointed. She'd psyched herself up in the elevator to tell him everything, even to ask him to go with her to St. Croix, though she knew he wouldn't.

"May I help you, Miss Bell?" the girl at the desk asked.

"The gentleman here a moment ago seemed quite—upset." Jane tried to say it casually.

There was a wry sound to the answer. "Yes, he was," the clerk said. "He seemed to feel we were hiding his fiancée from him. He left quietly so I guess Mr. Maxwell convinced him we weren't. He really appeared to be worried," she went on. "He said the girl's mother had died not long ago, and she was acting erratically."

Jane turned away to hide her dismay. So that was Howard's reasoning! Howard would never believe she was running from him.

She bought a magazine she didn't want, made sure a courtesy car would be available to take her to the airport in the morning, and forced herself to loiter in the lobby a little longer in case he came back—although her breath stuck every time the door opened. But he didn't. At last she went back upstairs.

She read forty pages of an Agatha Christie mystery and remembered nothing. She turned through the vacation brochures vacantly, unable to distinguish St. Croix from St. Thomas, Charlotte Amalie from Christiansted. At last she climbed into her new nightgown, turned out the light, and drifted into an uneasy sleep. But she'd made her decision: She was going!

The next morning she was halfway to the airport before she realized suddenly, *Good grief! I'm going to fly in an airplane!*

The terminal was located a fair distance from town. Her driver unloaded her suitcase, slammed the trunk lid shut, and asked, "Shall I carry it for you?"

"No, thank you, I can manage." Her eyes were already on the stone and glass building with the rows of aircraft on concrete behind it. She picked up her luggage, then suddenly realized he was still standing there.

"Oh," she said, shifting her dressing case and digging into her bag. "Thank you."

He grunted, "You're welcome," shoving the measly dollar tip down in his jeans. But what could he expect from a broad the help said made up her own motel bed?

Jane, unaware of his discontent, was already going in through the sliding doors. Her heart was beating quickly, and pausing beneath the blue glass diamonds of the high roof, she looked around in panic. She was early, she knew, but where in this expanse of white floor and soaring columns was the Air Illinois desk? And what was she going to fly in—one of those little planes out there—or that enormous thing with the green tail that stuck up over the roof?

From her booth by the steps to the café, Miss Evelyn Turner observed Jane Doorn. She had learned long ago to spot the timid advance of the neophyte. She tidied the lapels of her blue blazer, leaned across the counter, smiled, and asked, "May I help you?"

"Oh!" Jane said. She'd just then located the red, white, and blue logo overhead. "Yes. Yes, I think so. I'm going on a Limeberry Vacation and I was told to come here."

"Of course," said Miss Turner, picking up her clipboard. "Your name, please?"

"Jane Doorn. D-o-o-r-n."

"Right. Here we are. Now, will this be cash or credit card? Thank you," she said a moment later, putting the five hundred-dollar bills into a cash box. She took a bright yellow sticker with an emblem of berries on it, wrote Jane's name in black Magic Marker, leaned over, and slapped it on Jane's coat lapel.

"Come along now," she said, laughing, "and I'll introduce you to your fellow vacationers."

She came around the counter, slapped another sticker on Jane's luggage, and put it on a cart, then led Jane across the floor and up the steps to a balcony overlooking the runway.

Above paper coffee cups four pairs of eyes turned as they approached—two pairs like friendly puppies, one pair heavily lathered with peacock blue and red with weeping, and the last pair narrowed with appraisal.

"Miss Jane Doorn," said Miss Turner. "Mr. and Mrs. Willard Davis, Miss Melissa Grant, and Mrs. Marlene Von Fox."

"Ms.," said the owner of the appraising eyes coolly. "Ms. Von Fox." She nodded, recrossed sleekly clad legs, and went back to her *Vogue.*

Melissa Grant, who was all of seventeen, said "Hi" in a despairing voice and reglued her attention to the terminal doors—looking for someone, Jane decided, who probably wasn't coming.

The older couple, whom she at once classified as Tweedledum and Tweedledee, scooted their roly-poly fannies closer together so she could sit beside them and beamed a communal beam.

"Isn't this exciting?" chirped Mrs. Tweedle, otherwise identified as Madge. "We've never flown before."

"Neither have I," confessed Jane, and was rewarded with a momentary stare of disbelief from Ms. Von Fox. In less than five minutes Jane had a complete dossier on the Davises. Mr. Davis's line of work was hardware. They had four children and six grandchildren, and they were treating themselves to this trip for their forty-fifth wedding anniversary.

"I figure I'll buy Madge a bee-kini," said Mr. Davis and received a loving shove from his spouse, upon which they both giggled. Melissa mumbled, "Oh, gross!" and Ms. Von Fox kept her eyes averted from the domestic spectacle. Jane enjoyed it. She answered their questions readily: Where she was from; what she did; how bad the weather had been in her part of the country.

This display of mundanity quite clearly oppressed the chic Ms. Von Fox. On Evelyn Turner's cheerful summoning from the steps, she was the first to crisply slap her magazine shut, gather up her Gucci bag, and lead the group down from the mezzanine.

Miss Turner took them through security, put a folder of tickets in each hand, and opened the door to the cold, windy field. "Right out there," she said. "You'll be met in St. Louis, so don't worry. Mr. Nelson never fails. Have a nice trip!"

The wind had a bite as it swept across the huge flats of the airport. Jane pulled up her coat collar. By following the feet in front of her, she found herself mounting a short flight of steps.

73

Warmth came out to meet her. Raising her eyes, she discovered she was in a small, crowded tunnel with seats, some of them already occupied. A short, smiling girl was saying, "Welcome aboard. Sit here, please."

Jane took her place next to a sullen Melissa, who was tying knots in the fringe of her lumpy macrame shoulder bag. "I warn you," she said in a fierce whisper. "We made a vow, Dickie and me. We said that if they really kept us apart we'd kill ourselves on the stroke of twelve."

"Which stroke?" asked Jane, who sometimes liked to be precise.

Melissa hesitated. "The last stroke," she answered after deliberation.

Jane shrugged. "I hope you're right," she said. "It would be a shame to muff it." She wasn't as calm as she sounded; however, the girls she'd taught in Sunday school had always been threatening to do the most horrendous things, then usually just trotted off to eat pizza. Melissa did look upset—but also uncertain.

"Are you laughing at me?" Melissa demanded rudely.

"Not at all," Jane replied. "I just hate to have things come off like damp matches. Oh, my, look at that wing!"

Melissa turned and glanced out her window. "What about it?"

"It's shaking!"

"Of course. They just started up the left engine. You don't think I'll do it, do you?"

"Do what?" asked Jane, watching the wing and wishing it wouldn't vibrate so. "Oh. Of course I do. I just hope you don't mean to take a pill. People are likely to think you died of indigestion."

"I am not taking a pill!" Melissa said indignantly. "Dick and I bought twin knives. They have pearl handles. Oh, Miss Doorn, you haven't fastened your seat belt. Here, let me. And don't be nervous—we're quite safe. My father says the most dangerous part is driving to the airport."

Jane had no time to ponder on the extreme flexibility of youth. They had wheeled with a thunderous blast and began to lumber bumpily in an unseen direction. *I'm going to fly,* Jane thought in dismay. *And I can't even stand it on a rooftop!*

White-knuckled, she grabbed at the seat arms. The people about her were babbling as though nothing of great concern were happening. How could they?

Bump—bump—bump—was it going to be like this all the way to St. Louis? There! It was smoother now, although the pilot certainly had the front end up high. Of course he *knew* what he was doing. . . .

Now they were level again.

Jane took a deep breath. The stewardess was speaking into a microphone at the front of the cabin, smiling and talking about altitudes, time, and smoking while Jane waited patiently.

Melissa had pulled down the tiny tray on the seatback before her and was engaged in reapplying her eye makeup. Jane leaned over to ask when they would be taking off, and swallowed very hard as she looked out Melissa's window.

"The Mississippi," said Melissa, pointing out the window downward at a silver ribbon. "Oh, darn, clouds. Wait until we go through them. There—see it?"

Jane nodded, and leaned back. She felt foolish—yet excited, and pleased. Howard flew quite a lot—bankers' meetings, and so on. He was always talking about air pockets and sick bags.

The stewardess came by pushing a small cart with coffee and soda, and small baskets of gum and peppermints. Jane heard the Davises behind her ask for orange pop, and someone else complain about dry flights. Marlene Von Fox, across the aisle, took a soda. After the stewardess had gone, she quietly slipped a tiny bottle from her bag, dumped its contents in her cup, and gently swirled it. She met Jane's innocent gaze with one of pure hostility, raised the cup, and emptied the mix at one gulp.

Puzzled, and a bit daunted, Jane glanced away. Ms. Von Fox had a bright, enamel look, a sort of haggard elegance. Her legs were in superb shape, and well shod. Her opened coat showed a frontal elevation superior to even Jane's. She was also the only woman among the five or six on board with a hat—a smart turban that hid every lock of her hair and gave her an exotic aura.

An executive secretary, Jane decided, building her fantasy quietly. In love with her boss. Hopelessly, of course. Trying to forget. . . .

And I, she said to herself as she drank her own soda, *have had a five-year overdose of my mother's soap operas.*

The plane thrummed along efficiently. The Davises napped. People chattered. Ms. Von Fox asked for another soda, and again mixed it privately, tossing it off. Melissa took out a paperback about love's passionate something or other and began to read. Jane sipped her soda and relaxed.

"Fasten your seat belts, please, St. Louis is directly beneath us."

This time the nose of the plane went down instead of up, but Jane knew what was going on. She didn't exactly brace herself, but neither did she look. She had always believed that what you didn't see didn't hurt.

There was a bump, then the jogging began again. Some of the passengers were already in the aisle when the plane came to a stop. Jane waited until Marlene Von Fox and the Davises got up, then she followed them. From behind her, Melissa said chattily, "I like St. Louis. I might run away here. Except Uncle Trev wouldn't like it. On the other hand, maybe he would. I don't think he was too thrilled at having me traveling with him anyway —except my mother insisted. He needn't worry. I won't be around long enough to cramp his style."

Jane was barely listening. It was a little warmer in St. Louis, but there was ice beneath their feet as they were shepherded across the concourse, in through a sitting room, then up a carpeted ramp to a large open area where luggage was popping out of a chute and riding around a circle on a conveyor belt.

"Grab it fast," said Melissa. "There's mine." She plucked off a suitcase that was quite sizeable for a young lady contemplating her demise.

Jane saw hers, chased it, discovered it wasn't really hers, replaced it, red-faced, and found the proper one almost ready to disappear on the opposite side. A tenor voice said over a loud-speaker, "Limeberry Vacationers now boarding at Gate Five," and she hurried off, puffing a little. Where was Gate Five?

A hand touched her arm, and a soothing voice said, "Now, now, miss, not to worry. They'll wait for thee."

She glanced up at a shock of white hair, bright blue eyes, and an arm in a yellow coat, pointing. On the coat it said Limeberry Vacations. The wearer of the coat went on, "Right up yon, miss, and hang a left. Thee would see the sign, Gate Five. The boss is checking his sheep there. They'll nowt leave until all are counted."

Jane had little time to admire his unusual accent. She murmured her thanks and hurried on.

Clutching her suitcase, her dressing case, and her shoulder bag, Jane joined the line. The run and the anxiety had made her hot; she could feel her hair sticking to her forehead, and her hands felt moist and puffy.

Suddenly nudged in the back, she turned and saw that her attacker was a large golf bag. The owner murmured "Sorry" automatically. He was heavily tanned, with gray-frosted hair. Handsome brown eyes evaluated her briefly, dismissed her, and went back to the elegant turbaned head of Ms. Von Fox.

They were moving faster now. Jane could see the gate ahead, with attendants piling the luggage on carts, and someone tall in a Limeberry yellow coat checking names on a clipboard. The voice came over the loudspeaker again: "Please have your boarding passes ready, ladies and gentlemen. Please have your boarding passes ready."

As they moved forward, Jane began to juggle her dressing case and luggage to dig in her bag.

Good grief—where was it? She knew she'd put it there.

A deep, pleasant voice said, "Jane Doorn. Right?"

Jane answered, "Right." She looked up. Tom Nelson looked down.

He said, "You!" with little pleasure, then "Look out!"

But it was too late. Jane's suddenly nerveless fingers betrayed her. She made a mad grab, but both dressing case and bag fell

77

to the floor. The dressing case bounced but stayed intact. The shoulder bag upended rather magnificently. Makeup, change, Kleenex, pencils, keys, wallet, letters—it all slipped to the floor.

Crimson with shame, Jane dropped to her knees. Tom Nelson, sighing, dropped to his knees. After a moment, the gentleman with the golf bag put it down and dropped to his knees too. They began to retrieve the items.

Very humbly Jane said, "Here's my boarding pass."

"That's for down there. I don't need a boarding pass. I need a Jane Doorn."

"That's me."

Tom Nelson had risen to his feet, dusting his knees, and picked up his clipboard. "Now look—" he said, sounding grim.

Miserable with embarrassment, she mumbled, "That *is* me. That's my real name."

Tom Nelson shrugged. "Mine is not to reason why," he said, and checked it off.

Behind her, the tanned gentleman rose from his knees too. "Here, Miss Doorn," he said. He handed her a lipstick, three letters, and the check from McIlhenny and McIlhenny.

Appalled, Jane cried, "Oh, thank you! Thank you so much!"

The man looked amused. "Do you often carry things like that around?"

"No, no, I—I've just neglected to get it to a bank."

"Life is tough," said the man, and looked ahead. "Hello, Tom."

"Hello, Trev," said Tom with little pleasure. He took Jane's luggage and placed it on the cart. "There you go, miss . . . Doorn," and the way he said it made Jane feel like a criminal. "Give your pass to the woman at the door. And welcome to Limeberry Vacations."

Jane put one foot in front of the other. *Perhaps he isn't coming with us,* she said to herself. *Perhaps he just stays here and harasses other innocent people. I'm embarrassed and angry and—scared. I want him to go.*

I don't know why. But I do.

Behind her, Trevor Barry smiled at Tom Nelson, showing a

startling flash of white in his lean face. Softly he asked, "Anything for me this trip, Thomas?"

"No," said Tom, and the word came through his own teeth—set tightly.

"I'm not so sure," answered Trevor, his eyes focused ahead.

Tom thought they were on the elegant turbaned woman with the marvelous legs. They weren't. They were on Jane Doorn.

CHAPTER VII

Still hot-cheeked, and feeling tacky and disheveled with, undoubtedly, all her lipstick worn off and her hair stuck to her forehead, Jane moved on. Clutching her boarding pass and silently cursing the evil genie that seemed to delight in embarrassing her before Tom Nelson, she caught up with some familiar faces. The Davises were chattering happily to each other. Marlene Von Fox stood by, coolly aloof but watchful. Melissa was pretending not to look at a young man in air force blue, who was pretending not to look at her. Then suddenly she dropped her little cosmetics case, cried out "Uncle Trev!" and ran into the free arm of the gentleman with the golf clubs.

They hugged enthusiastically. He said, "Hi, kid, you're looking good."

"Uncle Trev, you can't imagine! Did they say what Daddy wanted to do to me? A convent! Can you imagine it! I was so relieved when Grandmama said come to her for Christmas—does she mind very much having me?"

All this came out in a tumble as she clung to his arm. He laughed, tousled her head, and kissed the top of it. "Slow down, young'un!" he said, laughing. "You know your grandmama better than that; she's delighted." He forbore saying that he was the one his mother wouldn't be thrilled to see. Susceptible ladies were not fewer, but rich ones were. He hadn't even made the cut at the tournament in Arizona, and taxes were due on the estate. No, Mother was not going to be happy to see him at all.

Can I be getting old, he asked himself, feeling the chill that had been nagging him recently. *Is the old snap going—the charm? What will I have left?*

Brace up, Trev—it's this kid, Ellen's girl, so full of youth it's almost indecent. Maybe some of it will rub off. . . .

His arm still around Melissa, he moved her on with the line, and his eye fell again on the leather coat and the darkly swirled head of Jane Doorn.

Money, he thought. *A wallet stuffed with green—and a ten-thousand-dollar check she's not even bothered to cash!*

But there are bad vibes with our Thomas. Very bad vibes. He needs money too. Mother says he and Karen are really scrambling to stay afloat.

Sorry about that, Nelson. I think I'll have a shot at her myself. Better than the elegant Elsie in the turban. I saw her eyeing me—like a praying mantis looks at lunch.

"Excuse me." It was the young man in the uniform. He was speaking to Trev but looking at Melissa. "You dropped this," he said.

"Oh!" said Melissa. She took her cosmetics case from his outstretched hand. "How dumb of me! Thank you. Are you going to Limeberry? Neat!"

Before Trevor discreetly dropped his niece's arm and moved ahead of them, communication was well established. His name was Michael, he had a four-day leave, and he was trying to get as far away from his base in Minot, North Dakota, as he could afford. Michael knew she was visiting her grandmama on St. Croix but staying at Limeberry, just around the beach, because Grandmama wasn't very well.

Trevor maneuvered himself to just behind Jane's leather coat, showed his boarding pass and managed to casually pull abreast of Jane as they went up the covered ramp into the airplane.

"Watch your step," he said quietly, and touched her elbow.

She started and looked at him. He saw a pair of blurred but pretty eyes the color of rich brown velvet and a set face. Not bad, though—and if the contours of the leather coat told the truth, the contents of the package might be nifty too. Still quietly, he said, "Don't mind our Thomas. He tends to shoulder the cares of the whole world."

"Oh, I don't mind," she said. "I don't mind at all."

The slender stewardess waggled the kiss curls of her blond hairdo at him. "Mr. Barry, welcome aboard."

"Thank you, Eve. Are you going all the way?"

"Just to Miami, worse luck." She hesitated, waiting for him to say we'll have to catch a drink between flights. But he didn't. He just went on, shepherding the girl in the leather coat.

Eve shrugged. That's the way Trev was. Self-centered as hell. But what an exciting man!

Behind her Jane heard the stewardess greeting more passengers. She moved forward and realized she was already aboard another plane. The aisle was wider this time, with more windows and seats on each side.

"Try this one," said Melissa's uncle, and turned her gently toward two empty seats on the right behind the wing. He loomed over her, pulling open a luggage locker above his head. "Shall I take your coat?"

He had already taken off and folded his coat. She nodded and he helped her with hers, folding it also, tucking both of them neatly overhead.

"Now," he said, and sat down beside her. He found that the contents of the package exceeded his original estimate. Both money and a body that made him catch his breath. Perhaps his luck was finally turning. . . .

Jane said in a questioning tone, "Melissa?"

He nodded across the aisle, where his niece and the young airman sat, oblivious of their noisy surroundings.

Despite her own unhappiness, Jane almost smiled. "She said she was going to kill herself at the stroke of twelve."

Not at all shocked, Trevor grinned—a slash of white teeth in a brown face. "Her mother indicated something of the sort," he said. "What was his name this year? Bobbie?"

"Dickie."

"Vows of undying fealty."

"Yes."

"If nothing better presents itself."

"So it appears."

"And it has appeared." He shrugged and thrust out a hand. "I'm Trevor Barry. I live on St. Croix. When I'm home."

"Not at Limeberry?"

"No, no. Limeberry is, as you know, a hostel. Mother and I

have a broken-down family home just around the beach from Limeberry. Within walking distance," he added, and his smoky eyes indicated the proximity could be nice.

A little flustered, Jane moved her bag around on her knees. Trev found her as pretty as a pink in his mother's old-fashioned garden.

Thomas Nelson had found her also, as he stood at the front of the cabin counting heads with the stewardess, who followed Tom's eyes and murmured softly, "He's been known to take the Miami layover literally. Would you like to place a bet? Or make a comment?"

"No bet," said Tom, and his voice was grim. "Only that it takes one to know one."

"Oh, nasty, nasty."

He ignored that. "I have my sheep," he said. "If you have yours, tell Andy to wind it up, and let's go."

"Andy's gone to the john and our second's still checking the weather. Have a cup of coffee, Tom, and I'll do the routine while we're waiting."

She took down the microphone and clicked it on, watching him from the corner of her eye as she did so. He looked so tired, so down. Of course there were only two-thirds of the Limeberry passengers he usually had and that was bad news. Tom and his sister were having real problems.

Eve held down the switch with her thumb. "I see we have Crystal Bell on board. She thinks she's disguised, but I knew her. Perhaps she'll bring you luck, Tom."

"I'd like to think so," he said, and let it go at that. But as Eve's throaty voice welcomed her passengers and went through the seat-belt oxygen-mask routine, he stared blackly into his coffee cup.

Jane Doorn indeed. Who did she think she was kidding?

I have to be nice to her. Damn. If she likes Limeberry, she could bring in a bunch of well-heeled friends. . . .

But that wasn't all. And he knew it.

How, he wondered, *can she give you that wide-eyed look like a little girl at a party when she's been around the Pike more times than Zebulon?*

At least she should be a match for Trevor Barry. . . .

At noon they served very good microwaved meals on little white trays. Jane, glancing past Trevor, saw his niece across the aisle happily munching on a cheeseburger and fries with apparently no thought for the stroke of midnight. Trevor said little, but he was a comfortable man to sit next to. After lunch he took out a paperback on golf.

"Got a problem with my backswing," he explained a little sheepishly.

Jane dug out her Agatha Christie, but other things distracted her—the play of sun and blue sky on the carpet of clouds, a picture so unreal she couldn't relate it to cities and people far below. It was like a never-never land.

Around her the other passengers seemed gripped in afternoon somnolence. Melissa napped, her head on Michael's shoulder. Behind Jane both of the Davises snored. Jane looked at the printed page and it danced before her eyes. She went to sleep wondering where Tom Nelson was. . . .

The light touch of Trevor Barry's hand wakened her.

"Miami International," he said and pointed.

The FASTEN SEAT BELTS and NO SMOKING signs came on. The aircraft canted gently downward. Jane, watching the concrete come rushing up, closed her eyes as the wheels touched with a sharp "Yeek! Yeek!"

"There went the beagles," said Trev, and then explained to her startled face, "That's what they call a good landing: killing the beagles. Look, we have half an hour in Miami. Let's collect the kids and take a walk. I know where there's a Baskin-Robbins, and I have a fatal weakness for butter pecan ice cream."

Tom checked them off on his list and stood a moment watching them go. There was a sick feeling at the bottom of his stomach, especially when Eve winked at him broadly.

"What did I tell you?" she said, gathering up her gear and fluffing her curls. "Have a good trip, Tom. I'll see you next time."

85

"Yeah," he muttered.

The fuel trucks rolled up, the new crew came on, and the next stewardess, a freckle-faced redhead, began welcoming the new passengers. Tom sighed, and went back to talk with his remaining tourists.

Marlene Von Fox had sat tight, wearing a pair of fierce, reflective sunglasses. She was next to the window, staring out at the glare of the sun on the concrete. She half turned as Tom bent to ask, "May I bring you something, Miss Von Fox?" He was suddenly aware that her smooth, high-cheeked face was strangely slack and that her voice was slurred. The woman was crocked! And they hadn't even served liquor. Where had she gotten it?

"Ms.," she was mumbling. "Ms. M' ver' particular about Ms. S' ver' good thing to hide behind. May I have some more soda?"

"What about a cup of coffee?" he answered gently.

A small smile curved her enameled mouth. "Dear man," she said, "don't you know all you'll get will be a wide-awake drunk? One more soda, darlin'. I am so tired. One more, and I promise. I'll go sleepy. When we get to your beau'ful par'dise, I'll be good as new."

She moved to pat his arm with a languid hand. Her Gucci bag clinked.

Tom shrugged, and brought her the soda. A three-hour nap might do the trick. Damn. Just what Karen needed right now: a lush guest.

A few moments later he stuck his head into the cockpit. Dan was already in his seat, whistling as he checked his instruments. Dan liked the island run; he had a girl friend on St. Croix. "Hello, Thomas," he said cheerfully. "Got a good bunch of snowbirds this time?"

"I hope so. How soon, Dan?"

"Oh, five minutes, give or take. Holy smoke, is that Trev Barry coming to board? He gets 'em younger all the time."

Tom glanced over the captain's shoulder. "One's his niece," he said glumly. He backed out of the cabin to Dan's "Oh, sure!" and took up his post at the door.

All four of them had ice cream cones. The niece and the air

force boy were giggling. Trev winked at Tom. Jane Doorn smiled tentatively, hesitantly. "I can't believe it," she said. "I know I sound like a tourist—but ice and snow in the morning and eighty degrees in the afternoon! It's like a miracle."

"We believe in miracles," said Tom in his best Limeberry voice. She did sound like a tourist. He knew Crystal Bell could dance; he hadn't known she could act too. All right, he'd go along with it. "One per day—so as not to dilute the product. Enjoy the flight. We should be in St. Croix late this afternoon. Oh, Trev—"

"What?"

"You're dribbling," said Tom, with immense satisfaction, and turned to greet the Davises.

When they took off the next time, Jane felt like a seasoned traveler. *It's incredible,* she thought. *I was hot down there. Really hot. And I saw palm trees—genuine palm trees, alive and growing in the ground—and flowers blooming, and people walking around in shorts. Now I'm hundreds of feet up in the air again and not scared at all!*

It's like a dream—and I'll wake up at home, listening to the furnace make funny noises and knowing I have to go to Howard's mother's for dinner. . . .

But I won't. I'm here. It's true.

She leaned back and let awareness seep into her bones—the feel of Trevor Barry's shoulder touching hers, the elegance of knife-creased trouserlegs, the sharp V of tanned, male throat disappearing into his shirt. A gold chain swung from his open collar as he leaned across to point out a fleeting glimpse of the Sun Coast condominiums down below. *He's charming,* she thought. *I've never met a man before who was charming. It's special. Different. And I probably should be wary, but I'm not. I like it. I wonder if Tom Nelson has noticed?*

The last thought came unbidden and unwanted. She flounced about in her seat angrily. Why was she upset? What did it matter if Tom Nelson had noticed?

As they winged their way in over St. Croix late that afternoon, the sun was a ripe apricot in the western sky, the sea a ripple of molten gold. Purple edged the island, turning its beaches to strips of white lace. Palms silhouetted their graceful fronds against the translucent horizon. The blackening hills shone with tiny crystal points of light.

Melissa disappeared with her uncle. Michael, bereft, attached himself to Jane. Tom put them both on board the old but brightly painted bus lettered LIMEBERRY COVE. He did seem, she noted, to be taking special care of Ms. Von Fox. Oh, well.

Darkness eased over the island as they nosed their way out of airport traffic. Jane could see very little around her. The road seemed narrow and rather hilly. The air was limpid and faintly perfumed. Once they drove right by a beach where dark bodies moved around small orange fires, and a clustered handful of bare sailboat masts pointed upward at the velvet sky.

It was warm—a mellow, caressing warm. Jane's leather coat felt heavy on her arm. She unbuttoned two buttons on the cranberry dress, baring more throat to the delight of the wind rushing in the windows.

Lights pricked the gloom ahead. The driver tooted his horn—a frivolous, happy tune on four notes. They swept grandly off the road onto a circle of white, crushed shell before a long, looming, hip-roofed building whose tall central door burst open hospitably. In the flood of light stood a slight figure wearing white slacks, with tawny hair caught high in a knot bright with red hibiscus. A gay voice called out, "Welcome to Limeberry Cove!"

"I'm Karen Sutton," the woman went on as her guests streamed across the yellow patch of light. "We're so glad you could come. Please stop by the desk; Adelaide has your room assignments. Don't change—you needn't tonight. Dinner will be in half an hour."

She does it so well, Tom thought affectionately, watching his sister smile, catch at outthrust hands, and make everyone feel special. *You'd never realize she's done it a thousand times—and hundreds since Rob's been dead. Bless her heart. I wish I could make things easier. . . .*

Marlene Von Fox was walking very straight, holding herself carefully erect. Tom steered her into the arms of old Hattie, a

88

specialist in problem guests, and turned to his sister. "Hi, Carrot. Everything cool?"

"Very. We just got the hot water going half an hour ago. Everything cool with you, Thomas?"

"So-so. Trev Barry came over with us."

"Cripes. He's not after one of ours, is he?"

"Could be. He says he's home for Christmas. We'll have his niece."

"We'll have her at night. I know. Her grandmother called me. She didn't say anything about Trev. Who is he chasing?"

"Crystal Bell."

"I didn't see that name."

"She's calling herself something else. But to Trev a rose by any other name still smells like money."

"Can she handle herself?"

"Very well," Tom answered grimly, remembering the clout on his jaw.

"Then not to worry," said Karen, a determined optimist. She spanked his behind. "Go change. You smell of smoke and cities. Addie has lime pie for dessert."

He started, then looked back. "Where's Toddy?"

"In bed, thank God. Old John took him fishing on Buck Island today and wore him out. You can see him tomorrow. Go on. You'll be late for dinner."

Tom had private rooms in the conical ruins of the old windmill beyond the gardens. As he strode down the familiar path, light suddenly streaked across the oleanders, outlining the tamarind trees. He turned and saw Jane Doorn silhouetted on her balcony in a bright square of light. She'd flung her arms out wide; the lovely, graceful line of breast and hip curved against the light. As he watched, unable to look away, she curled her arms again, hugging herself. Her uplifted face looked rapt, mystic, joyful.

Thoughts tumbled through his head: *Good God, she's pretty. I want her. This is ridiculous. I just met her three days ago. But the minute I touched her I wanted her and if she'd look at me now I'd be up the damned bougainvillaea hand-over-hand like a panting Tarzan.*

I'm nuts.

His hands betrayed him. They found a delicate spray of white oleander, snapped it off, and tossed it on the balcony.

Jane started and looked around, then picked it up. She saw him below her dimly, but recognized his tall frame, the square set of his shoulders, the pale line of his face, and she smiled.

"Thank you," she called in a very small voice.

"Compliments of the house," he answered roughly. Wheeling, he tramped on, opened the door of his apartment, walked inside, closed the door, and socked it hard with his fist.

"Damn it!" he said. "This can't go on!"

That Bell woman was still throwing him the old mating scent. He'd answered once, and got stung. He'd thought himself smarter than to try it again, but—damnation!

Hands off the guests. That was a tenet of Limeberry. Karen understood it, he understood it, and so did the rest of the help. Since that blonde had led him down the garden path two years ago, Tom had had no problem—until now.

Even standing in the dark, making firm resolutions, the picture of her, the curving line of her hips and breasts, burned on his memory. The smell of her, the taste of her . . .

In the dark he groped his way across the familiar carpet, found the fat scotch bottle on his bar, and took a good, sturdy wallop.

I don't need her, he told himself, wiping his mouth with the back of his hand. *It's an illusion. Treat her like a case of measles, and in three days she'll go away.*

Any man could hold out three damned days!

CHAPTER VIII

Jane awoke the next morning with a tremendous sense of antici-
pation. Birds were singing outside—strange, tropical birds.
Warm air and golden sun flowed through the slats of her window
shutters, fluttering the filmy curtains, bringing in a tingling smell
of cinnamon and salt. Yet she was cool and comfortable in her
white bed, curled beneath a crisp sheet.

Last night had been delightful. They'd sat at small tables in
the long dining room before a crackling fire. They'd eaten delicious food from stoneware plates laid on cloths of scarlet and
earth-toned batik. Karen Sutton told them about Limeberry
Cove, Frederiksted, Buck Island, and what they could do tomorrow—if they wanted to move at all.

Tom hadn't been there, but—Jane's eyes went to the sprig of
oleander stuck upright in a glass on her nightstand—that was all
right.

The flowers were there. They were real. It had happened. On
one tender, tropic night she'd stood on a balcony in soft, shimmering darkness and a tall man with handsome eyes had tossed
her flowers.

She slid pale feet to the straw matting, pattered over to the
louvered balcony door, and thrust it open. There she had her first
daylight view of St. Croix, and it was such a contrast to the dirty
ice and soiled snow she'd just left that she drew in a breath of
pure delight.

Below and to her left gleamed the sapphire jewel of a small
swimming pool, surrounded on two sides by round-arched arcades and on the other by allamanda vines clambering in profu-
sion over an old wall. From there a white gravel path wound
downward between palms and agave to where tough saltgrass
gave way to sand as pale as sugar. Water lapped over the sand,
water as green as sunlight on emeralds, water that deepened only

a few feet farther on, and changed to turquoise blue. In the distance other islands pierced the faraway mist.

It was a fantasy land. She was in it. And it all was hers for three whole days!

She showered in tepid water, but she didn't mind. Then came a delightful deliberation between slacks and shorts. Since Karen had said they would drive into Christiansted, the slacks won. Jane still hadn't enough nerve for the halter top, but the blue tennis shirt would do as well.

She went out to the balcony for one last look at the ocean. A movement by the pool caught her eyes. A coffee-colored woman in a bright headcloth was sweeping around the edge. She wore a heavily starched bungalow apron with shoulder ruffles that looked like wings. Her dark feet were thrust into loose shoes and she was humming.

From the cool shadows of the arcade came Tom Nelson. He led a small boy by the hand. They both wore swimming trunks, their bodies a contrast in lean brown litheness and chubby childhood. "Good morning, Addie," they said in cheerful unison.

"Mornin', Tom," Addie said. "Mornin', Tod."

"I dreamed about jumbies last night," the little boy went on seriously. "They said not to worry; your grandmama is going to be all right."

"Thank you, Toddy. Have a good swim."

Tod nodded. Trotting to keep up with his uncle's long stride, he followed him down the path. Her heart beating quickly, Jane watched them put their towels on the white sand, and walk into the water until nothing could be seen but their heads, like two wet seals.

This was such a fantasy. The temptation to let Tom Nelson be part of that fantasy was hard to resist. *It's only for three days,* her beating heart argued.

The gentle breeze shifted subtly, and bore to her the vanilla smell of the oleanders—but it also brought the jang-jang-jang of the breakfast bell. Giving herself a little warning shake, Jane left the balcony and went downstairs.

The dining room was alight with sun and bustle and the

cheerful chatter of a dozen guests. The buffet was stacked with heaps of butter-yellow scrambled eggs and bacon slices. Karen Sutton was pouring coffee from a steaming pot. She poured a cup for Jane as she slid into her seat next to the Davises.

"Good morning. Please help yourself. Did you sleep well?"

"Oh, yes!"

Karen held up one admonishing finger. She and her small son's large dark eyes matched remarkably, but although she was smiling, Karen's looked tired. "No, no," she said. "Never admit a positive or the jumbies will get you. Always say, 'not too bad,' or 'nothing worse.' "

Jane promised to remember. She took her plate to the sideboard and noticed that the chair occupied by Ms. Von Fox last night was empty this morning. As Jane heaped eggs and crisp crumples of bacon onto her plate, Melissa entered like a fresh breeze. Behind her her uncle waved and drove off in an ancient jeep with golf bags in the back.

"Hi," Melissa called cheerfully. "Gorgeous day! Uncle Trev has a golf match over at Fountain Valley, but he asked me to tell you 'Please hold your evening.' " This was to Jane, who started and blushed noticeably. To Karen she said, "Grandmama sends her respects and said to say the Weedwoman was going north on Centerline Road this morning if you wanted her for Louise."

"Oh," said Karen, whose eyes had been following Trev Barry out of sight, frowning slightly. "Yes, indeed, I do. I'll send Nat to find her."

Tom entered quietly, dressed in a denim shirt and blue jeans, his dark hair toweled dry. He nodded pleasantly to everyone in the room, his eyes sliding right over Jane. Karen hurried to him, and began to speak quietly. He grimaced and said, "I thought it was fixed. Damn. Okay, sis, I'll get right on it."

Karen squeezed his arm appreciatively, turned, and addressed everyone. "We'll get ourselves off for Christiansted in about half an hour. Walking shoes, everyone, and perhaps a sweater. At this time of year the wind off the water can be cool."

Jane, finishing her eggs, found the Davises embroiled in a

small argument. Mrs. Davis was saying, "Now, Willard, you're on vacation!"

"Well, it won't hurt to ask!" Mr. Davis answered. He crumpled his napkin and stood up, calling, "Tom!"

Tom came over, smiling, his plate in his hands. "Yes, sir?"

"What's the problem?"

Tom shrugged. "Not to worry," he said. "It's just the hot-water heater. Something minor, I hope."

Mr. Davis nodded, satisfied. His wife said a small "Oh, dear!" but he ignored her.

"Thought so," he grinned. "I ain't sold and repaired them things for thirty years without knowing the signs. Scale, likely. I know a dandy mixture to clean it right out. Finish your breakfast, young man, and we'll go have a look."

"Mr. Davis, I couldn't—"

"Sure you can," said Willard. He reached into his pocket, peeled off some bills, and thrust them in his wife's unwilling hand. "There you are, Mother. You shop for that there bee-kini. Surprise me. I'll just trot back upstairs and put on my coveralls."

Mrs. Davis watched him go out of sight. "Look at that," she said to Jane. "Happy as a clam. I knew he wasn't much for sight-seeing churches and old forts and such, but I had hoped . . . Oh, well. I hope you don't mind, Tom."

"Not at all." If Tom was dubious, he concealed it. He gave Jane a bright, professional smile and went to get more bacon. Jane, who had been shifting her eggs with her fork, thought, *He doesn't mind about me. Because he doesn't care about me. I'm written off. I wrote myself off back in that motel. I'm a guest. That's all. He probably didn't even recognize me last night on the balcony—he would have thrown that flower to any guest. It's part of the hospitality.*

Her ravenous appetite was gone though. Almost listlessly she scraped her plate, stacked it with the others, and followed Mrs. Davis out into the sunshine. With grim determination she took hold of herself and gave herself a mental shake. *Shape up, dummy! This is five hundred dollars' worth of good time. Fun, fun, fun! Enjoy!*

Clashing noisy gears, the bus finally pulled away from white-washed, tamarind-shaded Limeberry. A pleasant black man named Nat drove, and Karen stood beside him, her carroty topknot bobbing, describing what they were seeing. Jane was amazed at how soon she grew accustomed to driving on the left-hand side of the road. They rolled through lovely emerald hills and passed white beaches with pretty names like Grape Tree Cove and Grassy Point. Christiansted was clean and bright with bustling lines of people at Government House and the fort, and others strolling the waterfront, with its exotic flowering frangipani and the cluster of ship masts against the sky. There were cruise ships in at St. Thomas, Karen explained, and many tourists took the airboats over to St. Croix for the shops and the history. Jane enjoyed the luncheon at King's Wharf, and her respect for Karen increased as she never flagged in answering even silly questions, never seemed to push, but managed to move them all along. Yet somehow she had the sense that Karen was only going through set motions; her mind was elsewhere. Only at an old, restored sugar plantation mansion named Whim Greathouse did she really seem to come alive.

"I love this place," she said quietly to Jane as they chanced to stand together while the curator described the elegant dining salon with its tall windows and oriental carpet, the mellowed patina of Chippendale, and the many-candled brass chandeliers overhead. "It's what we would all love to have—what many of our ancestors did have. Limeberry was like this. My husband so wanted—" She stopped abruptly and looked away. "Retrospection," she said, almost to herself. "I can't afford it."

Feeling vaguely sorry, Jane asked, "Does anyone still live this way? I mean not with slaves, of course, but I know you still raise sugar cane and make rum. That does sound like money."

Karen smiled a little ruefully. "It does, doesn't it," she said. "Oh, yes. There are private houses that are—sumptuous. Trevor Barry's mother has one. Perhaps you've heard of Barrière Rum. That's Trev's family. As for money—well, for those born here, unfortunately, it seems to go out as fast as it comes in."

They moved with the passive crowd from cool depths into

sunshine, through the old Danish kitchen with its cavernous ovens and water filter, into bright warm day again, and along the flower-edged path to the sugar mill.

As they approached the tall, conical building with its huge sails, Jane said suddenly, "There is one of these at Limeberry! Except the windmill blades are broken."

Karen grinned, and her face was young again, impish. "We refer to it as picturesque," she admonished severely. "My brother lives in it. Look out!"

Her voice arrested Jane's foot. A green lizard gave them an anxious glance from bulging eyes and skittered to the shelter of a blazing bank of poinsettias.

Jane shuddered. "Are there many of those?" she asked.

"Only when you see them," said Karen. "There's probably been hundreds this morning you haven't seen. And they're harmless."

She moved away and began to gently herd her group back toward the bus. Jane followed, wondering if she'd imagined the sound of distaste in Karen's voice as she'd mentioned the Barrys.

But Karen's feelings didn't extend to Melissa, it seemed. When she'd decried the bus tour and announced her intentions of taking Michael down to the Limeberry beach, and seducing him there, Karen had only said, "Melissa, you'd shock your grandmother. She'd think you meant it."

"Who says I don't?" Melissa had challenged. Michael had turned deep pink and grinned. Then they'd all laughed, and Karen had sent them off with huge Limeberry towels and a cooler of soda.

Musing on this, Jane sat down in the bus next to Mrs. Davis, who rested her feet on her many newly acquired packages, a film of perspiration on her nose. She was fanning her face with the brim of an enormous straw hat.

"Mercy!" she said. "When we get home to Limeberry, I'm going right up and take off these shoes and have a nap. That Willard needn't think he's going to get out of dancing with me tonight!"

Jane smiled, and as Mrs. Davis began to count her packages,

she looked out the windows at the pageant rolling by—huge, towering monkey puzzle hedges, neat, hip-roofed cottages edged with croton and dripping with graceful wisteria, stone ruins overrun with insidious Ginger Thomas, whose yellow trumpets proclaimed the death of some householder's dreams.

Like Karen, Jane thought. *Was that it? Had Karen's dreams died with her husband? There was a ghost in her eyes. Now and then you could see it. . . .*

Would I feel like that if Howard died?

But, she rationalized swiftly, *I've never lived with Howard. We've never shared our lives.*

Back at Limeberry many of the guests felt as Mrs. Davis did. Exhausted from walking and the unaccustomed heat, they drooped off to their rooms. The rest scrambled into swim suits and trooped, laughing and chattering, down the path to the beach.

From her balcony Jane watched them. Below her the sapphire waters of the secluded pool gleamed deserted and tranquil. With resolution she stripped off her clothes, tugged on the brief, simple blue swimsuit, took a towel and a new bottle of suntan lotion, and padded quietly downstairs.

From the quiet of the arcade she peeped out cautiously. No one was there. Brave, now that she was certain of being alone, she went across the cement, and dragged a lounge chair into the full sun. The suntan oil smelled delicious. She dropped her straps and anointed herself as best she could, then stretched out on the towel-covered chair, her eyes shut. A great peace descended, and she went to sleep.

A few moments later Tom Nelson came through the arcades into the sunshine. His hair was wet with perspiration, he was unbuttoning his greasy shirt as he walked, and his weary mind was so fixed on the cool waters ahead that he almost didn't see Jane. When he did, he stopped short, and his dirty face was thunderous. He hated what the sight of her laying there did to him. How could she look so damned innocent, so delectably untouched?

For a moment he hesitated, and almost turned around. Then

his jaw tightened. The hell with that! For an hour in the grungy depths of the old boiler he'd been promising himself this dip in the pool. Jane Doorn was certainly not going to deprive him of it!

He stripped off the rest of his greasy clothes down to his swim trunks, dropping shirt and pants in a smelly heap on the pool side. He took a clean, quiet dive, swam to the opposite side, tossed the wet hair from his eyes, and grimly contemplated the female form recumbent on the lounge chair.

But the slight noise of his dive had awakened Jane. Her startled eyes had first taken in the dark head progressing across the pool, then the heap of greasy clothes on the cement. Indignation surging, she'd started to sit up, and grabbed at the side of the lounge, which went off balance and tipped her neatly into the water.

She gave one small squeak as she went under.

Tom laughed despite himself. It had all happened in a sort of slow motion. He laughed as she bobbed back up, gasping and flailing, and laughed again as she went down again. Then he suddenly realized: *The idiot can't swim!*

The pool was small. He crossed it like an arrow, and still laughing, he grabbed at her wet and pleasantly rounded body, saying, "All right, all right, I've got you!"

She didn't relax and clung to his chest as a rescued damsel should. She kept struggling, choking and sputtering, pushing at his shoulders with wet hands, almost, in fact, shoving him under. With a tremendous heave he finally succeeded in setting her up on the side of the pool, saying in an angry voice, "What is the matter? Are you crazy?"

He heaved himself out beside her. Her watery eyes went to his trunks. She said "Oh!" in a very small voice, and sat suddenly immobilized, crimson from her wet forehead down to the very nice curves revealed by the slipped straps of her suit.

Then he understood, and laughed. He lay back on the cement and howled. Between gusts and sputters, he managed to say, "I'm sorry—it's just so—you thought I was skinny-dipping! Oh, Lord! That's beautiful!"

He sat back up with an effort, wiping his eyes with a corner of his towel.

"I don't skinny-dip," he said, gasping. "At least not in this pool. Karen doesn't allow it. And I don't—repeat—don't dally with the guests. Karen doesn't allow that, either."

"What don't I allow?" asked Karen. She had emerged from the arcade with a glass of iced tea in her hand. Slipping off her shoes, she sat down next to them and dangled her bare feet in the water. "Oh, you've been swimming. Is the water warm enough? It got quite cool last night. Thomas Nelson, what is the matter with you?"

"Hysterics," said Tom amiably, at last able to control himself. "Total, utter, imbecilic hysterics. Born of fixing a boiler in company with a guy who's spent a hundred years in the hardware business but doesn't know a hot water heater from a Boeing 707. But it is fixed, madam. Your guests now have hot water. Lashings of hot water."

"Thank heavens for that," said Karen. She reached out and touched his dirty clothes. "Ugh. Have your swim then; you've earned it."

"What I've earned," said Tom, "I've had."

He stretched, stood up, gathered up his laundry, and said, "Afternoon, ladies," and went off whistling. They both watched him, tall and tanned, swinging past the cassia trees with their heavy yellow flower clusters and the stately spikes of the white-belled century plants. A turn in the path took him from sight.

Jane sighed. It was a choky, funny sigh; she tried to keep it back but couldn't. Karen turned, looking at her sharply.

"My idiot brother," she said gently. "Did he offend you?"

"Oh, no!" said Jane, and grimaced. "I'm just . . . embarrassed. You see, I don't swim. And I fell into the pool. He pulled me out, but I'm the one who's the idiot. I thought—" and she blushed again.

Karen rescued her. "Never mind," she said. "It can't be important. Let me see—you're with the Quincy group, aren't you? Tell me how awful it is back in Illinois."

Gratefully Jane took the bait, and Karen led her on with deft questions. She'd had a strong sense of something—she couldn't define what, but definitely something—as she'd come upon these two. And she was worried about her brother. Tom had been severely stung by a strawberry blonde two years ago; since then he'd had a tough, cynical attitude toward women—and this girl seemed unmistakably vulnerable.

As Jane talked Karen was appalled at just how vulnerable she really was. *My heavens,* she thought, *this is a downy chick! I suppose I'm not responsible for her, but I feel that I am.*
. . .

And there's really no man to pair her with. No safe man. Damn Tom—does he have to be so handsome? He doesn't realize how attractive he is. Well, yes, he does. Unfortunately. I'll just have to speak to him.

A soft voice from the shady arcade said, "Mrs. Sutton?"

Karen turned. "Yes, Addie?"

"The Weedwoman's come. She's gone to see Grandmam."

"Good. I know she'll make Louise feel better. Take her tea, will you, Addie? And some rum cake. A nice tray. Call me before she goes."

"Weedwoman?" Jane said curiously, "I gather someone is sick. Is Weedwoman like medicine man?"

Karen smiled. "A little," she said. "She's really a herbalist—she knows hundreds of them, probably every one on the island. And she knows how to use them. She's sort of an unlicensed practitioner, I suppose. And she can't help old Louise—at least not very much. Louise is ninety-nine, and has been here forever. She was my husband's housekeeper, and his parents', and his grandparents before him. Addie is her granddaughter, Nat, her nephew. The whole fabric of Limeberry seems bound up by old Louise. It won't seem the same when she's gone. Shall I oil your back, Jane? It's getting pink."

Jane turned gratefully. As Karen doused her with tanning oil, she caught sight of a moving figure on the balcony beyond them. "Oh, there's Ms. Von Fox. She didn't go with us today, did she?"

Karen gave the tall figure only a cursory glance. "No. She's here to—rest, I gather. Not sight-see. She probably won't be very social." *Unless you're male,* she added to herself. *If I ever saw a female barracuda, there's one. But the money! And how we need it! What I need on my staff is a good old-fashioned gigolo.* . . .

As if on cue, Trevor Barry appeared. He was tanned and immaculate. The sun glinted frostily on his silvering hair, and having had a very lucrative morning on the golf course, he exuded extreme self-satisfaction. He said, "Good afternoon, charming ladies."

Jane opened her eyes at the sound of his rich voice, but she didn't stir. Karen answered a little shortly, "Hi, Trev. Melissa's on the beach."

"Long may she stay there," replied Trev, grinning. He stretched his long length in an adjacent lounge chair, pointed a trimly shod foot and touched Jane's bare thigh. "'Tis not avuncular companionship I seek, but that of this drowsing beauty here. May I take you to dinner, Jane? I promise dining, and superior wining, and a personal order of moonlight over Frenchman's Reef."

"No," said Karen before Jane could answer. "I've my tables made up for this evening, and you're not going to break the number."

She saw the swift spark of anger in Trevor's eyes, but he concealed it suavely. This alarmed her more. There was quarry here he did not choose to surrender. But—of all people—Jane. Jane, pinching her pennies for this three-day vacation. Jane the naive little shopgirl. Why? Then, as Jane slowly sat up, swinging her legs to the cement, self-consciously winding her towel to cover her shoulders but succeeding only in accenting the sensuous curve of soft, full breasts, Karen thought to herself, *You idiot, you know why!*

But there had to be some other reason. Trev was a notorious womanizer, but he rarely indulged himself with poor women. He couldn't afford to.

Jane was following Karen's lead. Beneath the towel her heart was jumping. Trevor Barry frightened her a little. He was so confident, so sure of himself. There was something of the latent tiger in him. Even the way he sat, leaning carelessly back, dangling one foot, his golf shirt opened to show the tanned column of his throat, the brown muscles of his arms, the flat belly, the shine of silver in his hair—all those things created a strange pull inside her, a pulse beat that was different from her helpless reaction to Tom Nelson, yet in an alarming way the same.

"Thank you," she said hesitantly. "I really shouldn't. Not this evening."

He shrugged. Getting out a cigarette and lighting it, he looked straight at Karen over his cupped hands. "All right. Tomorrow then. Come with me over to Charlotte Amalie town. That's on St. Thomas. I'll show you the shops. Then Mother would be delighted to have you to tea tomorrow afternoon at Barry Greathouse. Melissa will be there too, so surely your mother superior can't object to that."

Jane felt Karen stiffen beside her, and wasn't sure why. Shopping sounded innocuous, and an afternoon at the Barry home might be interesting. Karen had said they had one of the few authentic old homes left. And if Melissa was also going to be there . . .

"It sounds neat," she said. "I'd like that."

"Great," he answered, inhaling deeply and blowing blue smoke upward. "I'll tell my mother. We'll look forward to it. Care to join us, Karen darling? It's been a long time."

It was a direct challenge. Karen's mouth set, but she met his eyes without flinching. "No," she said.

"In the morning then. About nine."

"Fine," said Jane. But despite herself, she suddenly shivered.

Karen said swiftly, "You're cold. Run and get some clothes on and I'll take you to meet the Weedwoman. I think you'll enjoy her. Make yourself comfortable, Trev. Would you like a drink? I'll send Addie."

"No, thank you. I would like Melissa now, if you can find her."

"Of course. You may have to take Michael also."

"I suppose, although you might mention that someone named Dick is going to call at seven."

Karen nodded and almost whisked Jane away. *Like a protective mother hen,* Trevor thought grimly. *She's got the wind up all right. Well, it won't do her any good. . . .*

Damn it all, he said to himself in sudden anger, *when have I not been discreet? Karen knows better than that.*

A shadowy movement on his right caught his eye. He turned, and saw Marlene Von Fox coming to the edge of the pool. She wore a black thong bikini. Her body was fit and beautiful, with superb dancer's legs. A mass of pale hair tumbled softly down her honey-colored back. She raised both arms to knot it on top of her head and the points of her breasts in their ridiculous black scraps rose breathtakingly.

"Hello," she said.

"Hello, yourself," said Trevor, instantly responding to her blatant invitation.

Jane had gone out on her balcony to toss away the sprig of oleander. She saw them below, saw Marlene Von Fox in her brief bits of black, saw Trevor's tanned hand slide knowingly down her graceful, toast-colored back as he said, "Eight o'clock."

"Eight o'clock," she answered.

Trevor smiled, and walked away as his niece came running gaily up the path from the beach. She hugged him and they went off, arm in arm. Marlene Von Fox arranged herself on Trev's lounge chair, moved the black scraps so that her bared breasts shone brown and Polynesian in the sun, put on dark glasses, and lay perfectly still.

Aghast, Jane stared down. *Doesn't she know someone will see her?* was her first thought, swiftly followed by, *She doesn't care; perhaps she's even hoping—then, good grief—she's brown all over! Everywhere!*

Her cheeks pink, Jane withdrew swiftly, the oleander still in her hand. Unthinking, she thrust it back in the glass.

Below her, in the whitewashed corridor, Karen forestalled her brother. "Ms. Von Fox," she said grimly, "is advertising her talents by the pool. I've warned off the help, but you're too big to spank."

He grinned. In a fresh shirt and jeans, he felt better. "As I told the woman who calls herself Jane Doorn, I don't dally with guests."

"You told her what!" gasped Karen.

But he was looking beyond her. "There's Miss Uba and her weed basket," he said. "Is Louise . . ."

He let the word trail off but his brows were drawn. Tom loved old Louise; everyone did.

Karen patted his arm. "I don't know," she said. "I told Addie to give her tea in the little sitting room. Let's go ask her."

Together they walked down the corridor and out of sight.

CHAPTER IX

Jane awakened very early the next morning. She heard people singing. The sound drifted in through the louvers of her balcony door on the pearl gray mists of the newly dawning day so softly that she wasn't certain she'd heard it at all before it ebbed away and was gone.

She lay very still and listened. But now there was nothing but morning sounds—the faintest whisper of green water against the shore, the cheerful squeaks of yellow-breasted birds bobbing in the oleanders, and the soft fall of footsteps in the hallway.

The steps went into Marlene Von Fox's room next door. There followed the audible click of a lock, the separate noise of two shoes falling to the straw matting, a deep, luxurious sigh—then nothing more.

She probably had an early morning swim, thought Jane. She stretched, yawned, and a similar idea took hold of her. Not a swim, but a walk all by herself, along the white curve of the beach in the morning cool, the spaceless quiet—where she could think.

Jane dressed quickly, pulling on yesterday's slacks and the halter top, noting with pleasure what yesterday's sun had done to her winter pallor.

Everything downstairs was still. The stones of the arcade were damp and chill. Morning moisture turned the leaves of the barrier hedge to dark shiny green. Beyond the point of making disturbing sounds, she slowed her steps and walked at a leisurely pace, breathing in the cool, fresh air with its tang of salt and vanilla, avoiding the patches of sanseveria and croton, and the prickly outcroppings of cactus that pierced the tough saltgrass. Palms fringed the edge of the sand. Fallen brown fronds crackled beneath her feet as she sauntered onto the white curve of the cove itself. A long, narrow dock pointed toward the sea, and a cluster of beach umbrellas looked like bright mushrooms. She turned away from them to the left and headed toward the jumbled pile of wet, dark rocks.

The sand was wet. Impulsively she stopped, pulled off her canvas sneakers and walked on, delighting in the feel of the cool wet beach on her bare feet. Two brown sandpipers skittered along the water's edge before her, and overhead a frigate bird wheeled in huge, sweeping circles.

If I don't look at the beach umbrellas, she told herself, *or the roof ridges behind me, I could be a Robinson Crusoe. . . .*

Such thoughts were hardly what she had come here to consider. But it was hard. Snow and sleet, ice-jammed eaves—those meant nothing to her now. Nor did Howard, with his silky moustache and plump cheeks, doling out change from that awful change purse.

How she hated that thing! Why couldn't he carry loose money in his pocket like other men?

She knew why. His mother said keys and change wore pockets out. His mother had bought him the clasp-topped purse.

Still, she ought to write to him—or something. But she couldn't.

Why hadn't she realized that one taste of freedom would have such dangerous repercussions? Her entire outlook was changing —her manner, her tastes, her ideas . . .

And it wouldn't do. It just wouldn't do. Because no matter how she changed, she still had to go back. There was the truth. There was the reality.

She was near the towering pile of rocks now. Looking up, she suddenly saw that they were occupied. Tom Nelson was looking down at her.

His denim-clad shoulders hunched, his brown arms on bent knees, he sat on the flat top of one of the boulders. He had been staring out to sea. Now, of course, he wasn't.

Good grief, Jane thought humbly, *he'll think I saw him and came over. I didn't see him at all, but he'll never believe that. He'll have to be nice to me because I'm a guest, and he'll hate it. Me too. But what can I do?*

Tom, indeed, had his be-nice-to-the-guests look on. Whatever feelings he'd had on her approach had been stifled—he hoped—and he wished Jane a good morning in his deep, pleasant voice. "Come up," he said, and put down a tanned hand.

There seemed to be no way out. Meekly she accepted the warm, strong clasp and, clinging as though to a lifeline, she clambered up to his side. He'd spread his denim jacket to sit on in lieu of wet lichen; he gestured for her to share the space. She obeyed, then grimaced as he continued to scrutinize her.

"I didn't expect company," she said awkwardly. "I just came out—I mean—I haven't my face on yet."

Gravely he replied, "The original is very nice." He'd been thinking just that. She'd lost the tired, harried look. Even without the professional gloss, her skin had tone, and the morning breeze had put a tint on her cheeks. What the halter exposed—which was also very nice—was turning a velvet apricot color. *Careful, Thomas,* he added to himself, and turned back to the sea.

She sat beside him, acutely aware of his broad, denim shoulder touching hers, and looked at their feet paired on the stone. His were brown and bare beneath turned-up pantlegs. Hers were sandy, with tan and white stripes—the results of yesterday's sandals—and one red nail was chipped. It seemed a glaring fault in the perfect morning light, and hastily she put the other foot over it.

The sun pushed a tentative silver rim over the mounds of a faraway island. Beautiful color began to creep across the gleaming sea.

Jane sighed, and it was almost a sob. Ashamed, she turned it into a cough, but she hadn't deceived Tom and she knew it. "Oh, I hate to leave," she said, "I hate to even think about leaving."

"Stay, then." He said it casually, quietly, not even looking.

"If I only could."

He almost looked at her then. Her voice was so full of woe. *Hot damn,* he thought ruefully, *what sort of problems does she imagine she has? Not men; that's for sure.*

"I hate to leave too," he said.

Beside him she started. Timidly she asked, "Why should you go? You live here."

He sighed and rubbed his eyes, which were very, very tired. He'd been up all night. "When my brother-in-law died," he said flatly, "I took a year's leave to come and see if I could help Karen bail this place out. Now—well, frankly, we're not making it. I was just sitting here thinking that maybe if I went back to work, my salary would help us hang on at least another year."

"What—" she hesitated, not wanting to intrude, then plunged on anyway. "What do you do—when you do it?"

The breeze was riffling the dark hair across his forehead. He scraped it back with an absent hand. "Engineer," he said. "Construction. Bridges, roads—you know. I loved it until I came to St. Croix. Now I'm afraid I've got island fever. And I realize they can't keep my job open forever—even if it is my uncle's outfit. My mother was a McIlhenny."

The name made a familiar sound in Jane's ear. She started to comment on her recognition of the name. But she broke off when Tom said softly, "Look. Down there."

"Where?" She saw nothing.

"There," he repeated, and put a hand to the back of her head, turning it.

Beyond him old sea grapevines clustered along the sandy shore and climbed the rocks. Through them waddled a very proud and important mother duck. Plop! she went, into the wind-ruffled water, and plop, plop, plop behind her went three small balls of fluff.

"Aren't they sweet?" Jane exclaimed.

Tom had suddenly become aware of the soft hair beneath his fingers and her breath on his own lean cheek. He dropped his hand abruptly.

"Yeah," he said, a little tightly. "You see a lot of them this time of year."

She followed the ducks out of sight, then looked a long time at where they'd been.

Uncomfortable, Tom stretched out his long legs and in his best humor-the-guests voice, said, "There's quite a variety over on

Buck's Island. Are you a bird watcher? Karen can arrange a nice jaunt over there for you."

"No," she said. She didn't understand the change in him. They'd been talking almost like friends. Now he was suddenly distant again. He'd even moved his shoulder away. And bird watching! Is that how she looked to him—like a prim and proper robin counter? She'd show him she had other things to do! She said sweetly, "My day is filled anyway I'm afraid. Trevor has asked me to go shopping, then to tea with his mother at Barry Greathouse. I am really looking forward to it."

He not only stiffened, he went absolutely rigid.

"Shopping," he said. "And with Trevor. In Charlotte Amalie, of course." *Of course,* he thought. *Trevor knows those shops well; he gets a sizeable kickback from most of them, you little idiot! But I suppose you can afford it. And maybe you can handle Trevor too.*

She knew she'd made him angry, and perversely it pleased her, although she didn't know exactly why he was angry. "I understand they have a lovely home," she said.

"Yes," he replied.

Above them on the hill the breakfast bell jangled. They both stood up. Tom picked up his jacket, Jane, her shoes. He slid expertly down the rock and held up his hands for her.

"Be careful," he said politely.

Did she stumble, or did she deliberately fall? Surely she was bright enough not to use the same gambit again. And surely he was bright enough to resist.

But there she was, catapulting forward, and there he was, catching her in his arms, that terry halter with its lovely and well-remembered contents pressed against the open front of his shirt, his heart thumping inside his chest and her mouth a soft, rosy circle right beneath his own. Every man has his limits. Tom had reached his.

He kissed her mouth, her throat, that lovely, breathtaking valley between her breasts, kissed her until she was shaking and clinging, until they both were, until in near agony he muttered against the barely covered mounds that so enticed him, "All right, lady, you win—how do you want it?"

109

She was hardly capable of answering. Her entire singing body was crying out *Don't stop, don't stop*, and she welcomed the husky sound of his voice against her breasts. But his words stunned her.

No sweet tenderness? No love? Just how do you want it?

She gasped as though ice water had been savagely dumped on her head. She yanked away, and the move was so unexpected that he let her go. Her face flamed, and she panted, "Oh! Oh!" It was such an inadequate word, but all she could say.

"Oh," he said, and it was no longer inadequate when followed by, "I see. I suppose we mustn't ruin the day for Trevor." It came out grimly through his teeth, and his face was set in iron. No man likes to look foolish. He not only looked foolish but he was furious. "Then get on up that hill, Miss Bell," he said, "and stay out of my way—because, by God, I warn you: guest or not, next time I won't be so easy to get along with!"

CHAPTER X

Addie had gone ahead and cooked breakfast. Grandmama would have wanted her to; she'd never been one to shirk her duty. Karen had sent Nat into Frederiksted to see the pastor and make the funeral arrangements. Until he returned, there wasn't anything else to do, and guests get hungry—especially when the sorrow isn't their own.

As she rang the small triangle, Addie saw one of the guests coming up the path, Tom trailing far behind. My, the lady looked unhappy. Had Tom done something wrong? Addie couldn't believe that. Tom was such a good man. He'd stayed with Grandmama all night, clear through to the first crack of dawn, when she'd given that one last, soft breath, swept them all with her old eyes, and died.

Addie's own eyes clouded with tears; still, resolutely, she said to Jane as she approached, "Morning, miss. I hope you slept well."

"Nothing worse," replied Jane, showing she remembered. At least she could do something right. Hoping Addie took her sharp breathing as a result of the long hill, she smiled at her carefully and went on by.

Breakfast was the last thing she wanted. *This is my middle day,* she said to herself desperately, *my middle day of vacation— and I can't let him spoil it! I mustn't! I have to erase this morning —and I will. I will!*

But I'll never wear this terry halter again. . . .

This morning the water in the shower was fiery hot; nonetheless, Jane scrubbed both body and hair as though she'd been contaminated.

Then, her head in a towel, she splashed on after-bath scent lavishly, filling the room with subtle sweetness. She felt an almost wicked guilt. Her mother had not approved of perfume.

The strapless underwire bra was new.

111

I wonder what Mother would think of this, she pondered, squirming into some sort of dubious comfort. But she didn't actually wonder. She *knew.*

Bending closer to the mirror, she put on basic makeup carefully, smeared her eye shadow, tissued it off and tried a second time. The bra poked her, and she wriggled again, finally achieving a comparatively painless adjustment. If she was going to wear that sundress without the jacket, she had to have the strapless bra.

For some reason an old memory came back: ten-year-old Jane in a new organdy, puff-sleeved dress—a dress ruined by lumpy, heavy winter underwear with sleeves rolled up and stuffed inside the puffs, and the top two buttons of the neck pinned under with enormous safety pins. Mother had said it wouldn't show. But it had.

How well Jane remembered the humiliation of that day! She remembered her mother saying virtuously, "My daughter is not going to run about naked."

Now the daughter looked at herself in the mirror. She saw breasts no longer repressed, but lifted and shaped by a couturier's best art, a tiny waist that swelled to very feminine contours, silkily and briefly covered, round legs freshly smoothed and tanned. She touched her body and tried to conjure up her mother's feelings, but she couldn't. Instead she found herself wondering if her mother had ever known a Tom Nelson.

No. Mother had lived in a box too, and whatever else it was, it had been respectable. Just as Howard was respectable.

Jane shivered, and turned away. There was nothing to be gained by looking. Or remembering . . .

This was the middle day of Jane's vacation. A fascinating man was coming to take her out. She was going to have a good time. Grimly she repeated that to herself.

All her trouble with the makeup and the bra and fastening the white, poppy-splashed sundress was worth it when Trevor came in the door.

"Charming," he said. "Absolutely, unequivocably charming!"

No one had ever before called plain Jane Doorn charming. It

helped make up for the morning. Embarrassed, but pleased, she said, "It's new. I've been dying to wear it."

Trevor smiled, tucked her hand in the crook of his arm, and patted it.

"I'm talking about the whole package," he said. His mind was swiftly revamping his plans for the day. From hair to shoes this girl breathed money, class. He'd better take her where all the pukka sahibs gathered, show those high-finance snobs that Trevor Barry could still manage very well. And maybe get a few creditors off his back.

He felt much better as he escorted Jane out to the convertible Porsche on the sunny driveway. He'd been a bit late. Marlene Von Fox had shunned the brighter lights of the island last night, but her tastes in wine had been as lengthy as expensive. And her prowess in bed, to which they had rather quickly progressed, had proved not only innovative but exhaustingly athletic as well.

Jane Doorn should be a sweet respite as well as profitable. He was glad he had borrowed the Porsche.

Good grief, Jane Doorn was saying to herself, *I'm in a convertible! Never before in my life have I been in a convertible.*

Nervously she settled herself and tried hard to smile casually as Trevor, in spotless white pants and shirt, slid in close beside her. He started the engine. It purred.

"Nice baby," he said, flashing a blatantly audacious grin at Tom Nelson, who was scowling down on them from the edge of the roof reservoir where he was cleaning out leaves.

They took one of the air boats to St. Thomas—an exciting trip for Jane, who loved the sound of the spray and the lunge of the big twin-engined "goose" breaking water. Then Trev found a little table in a small café overlooking the bustling waterfront. They sipped coffee, and Jane watched, round-eyed, at the boatloads of people shuttling to and from the huge cruise ships anchored in the harbor, at the surging masses of chattering, camera-hung, vacation-clad tourists. They were shouting, posing, laughing, and clicking pictures. They wore absurd hats and absurder costumes, and came in all shapes and sizes, displaying every degree of sunburn.

Trevor, leaning back, his legs crossed, was watching Jane. What was this infant's background? Midwestern, of course. Newly rich? Perhaps. He found her total lack of artifice refreshing. And disarming.

But not too disarming, of course. He could allow himself to be amused, but he could not allow himself to be diverted. "Taxes," Mother had said just this morning. "Taxes, Trevor."

Forcing his mind from the subtle sweetness of Jane's flesh to the fat contents of her purse, he leaned forward, aware that the motion bared a very bronze and manly chest.

"What would you like to do?" he asked. "What would you like to buy? I have friends in some of the shops; we'll make sure no one rips you off."

Jane thought of Howard, and frowned uncertainly. She could spend a hundred dollars, no more. "What is there?"

"My darling, almost anything your little heart desires. All island-made articles are duty free, and good old Uncle Sam allows you two hundred exemption on the rest. Come along before these pesty cruise-ship people gobble up the good stuff."

He arose, stretching like a lithe tiger, carelessly tossed down some crumpled dollars from his pants pocket, and held out his hand.

Jane thought poignantly: *No clasp-topped coin purse!*

She got up also, found his brown fingers cool, his grip loose and companionable. Swinging their linked arms like children, they sauntered off the docks into the bustling, steep-pitched streets and tiny, whitewashed, fret-worked shops of Charlotte Amalie.

The noise was incredible—a potpourri of voices from every part of the globe, counterpointed by the yaps of indignant car horns, and the persistent singsong of vendors hawking their exotic wares. Jane found herself in small, dim, cool shops where crystal and china gleamed, where unstrung pearls poured onto black velvet, where linen looked as fragile as frost and leather had the patina of mahogany. They wandered through narrow, queer little streets. Everywhere sleek clerks in fashionable sport

114

dresses, chains as thin as wire around their necks, and salesmen in immaculate open-throated shirts said, "Good morning, Trev."

He knows everyone, she thought in admiration. She found herself buying Mother Van Tassel a linen tablecloth with exquisitely drawn threads, and Howard a wallet, beautifully made and lined, and for herself a crystal Lalique paperweight shaped like an owl, so elegantly fashioned that she couldn't resist it. She spent far more than a hundred dollars and declared herself through—until she saw the hand-batiked sarong wraps and the strings of lovely amber jewelry.

At last, conscience-stricken and not daring to add up what she'd spent, she collapsed on a bench beneath a fountain of graceful wisteria blossoms, gasping, "I must stop! I must!"

Trevor grinned down at her and shrugged. "Why?" he asked. "Aren't you enjoying it?"

"I am. Oh, I am. That's the problem. Trev, have you any idea what I've spent?"

"Who counts?" he asked. But he'd had a very good morning. Perhaps he had pushed it far enough for this day. Besides, by now everyone who was anyone was gathered at The Club for an aperitif. Jane would raise the Barry stock a little more among the nabobs.

Even in the short time it took them to get settled at a seaside table, Trev could sense that word was out about this girl in the poppy-strewn dress who disdained credit cards for greenbacks. There was warmth in some of the greetings—which had been noticeably cooler since his poor showing on the golf tours this year.

Their aperitifs came in small, slender glasses. Jane took a cautious sip, and tried hard not to make a face.

Trev laughed. "It's an acquired taste," he said. "Like olives." He leaned closer to point out things in the harbor, his arm resting casually but proprietorially across her shoulders.

Her nervousness returned. The grotesqueness of the whole thing had struck her: Jane Doorn, having a drink on a club veranda by the sea with this handsome man-about-town. What

115

was she doing here? Jane Doorn was even too inept to ask for the ladies' room without blushing.

And she did need to ask for the ladies' room. Whatever did one say? No one powdered noses anymore!

She knew what Sally always said: "Anyone else for the can?" Jane tensed, just thinking about Sally. *Use your eyes, idiot,* she told herself. *There are other women here; they have to go somewhere!*

She glanced at Trevor and found him looking back. There was a half grin on his face.

"Around the corner," he said. "Then left. The sign says MER-MAIDS—which is the management being cute. Don't stay too long, or we'll miss the boat."

Everyone watched her as she went, and watched her as she came back. Satisfied, Trev signed the tab, looking the waiter defiantly in the eye, and they left, his hand gently on Jane's elbow.

A disquieting thought marred Trevor's enjoyment of the airboat trip back. As the Porsche purred its way along Centerline Road, he let it surface.

This Jane was a creature of contraries. She could be as much a schoolgirl on vacation as his niece. Then the vane would swing and she'd be as prim as a daisy. Another turn and she seemed as sensuously aware of him as he was of her. This was not the manner of a girl from the debutante genre. Yet, she had money—he'd seen it—money in checks (at least one check) and long green stuff. But why cash—cash for everything?

Good God, he thought in abrupt discomfort, *what if she is a schoolgirl who just ran off with the clean-towel fund? Don't joke, Barry. This could be serious. Girls her age have embezzled before. Find out!*

He glanced at her quizzically; she saw him looking and gave him a shy smile. Her hair was blowing back, her cheeks were pink, and her eyes sparkled.

"Hey," he said, "I hope you realize you raised the economy of St. Thomas about eighteen percent. Don't you ever use a credit card?"

She closed her eyes and let the limpid air rush across her face. "I don't have any with me." How easily that came out! she thought. She was turning into an accomplished liar. "Nor my checkbook either. In fact when my car broke down in Quincy, I was scared to death!"

"What did you do?"

"I called Howard."

"Who's Howard?"

"My . . . banker. He transferred some funds for me."

His keen ear had caught the hesitation, but he only grinned. "I wish I had a banker that obliging."

"Howard is very nice." She said it firmly, as though to convince herself, he thought. This Howard dude would bear looking into. But he believed her, and was relieved.

There was a rusting old Plymouth station wagon ahead, grinding along in second gear and jammed with fresh, long green guinea grass. He wheeled around it; the motion opened Jane's eyes. "What will they do with that?" she asked curiously.

He shrugged. "Feed their horses probably. There's still a lot of horses on St. Croix."

The road curved, and Jane found herself looking out over the descending roofs of a cluster of condominiums that marched toward the incredible jewel blue of the sea. But Trevor was frowning.

"There's a lot of that too," he said, indicating the condominiums. "And more coming, I'm afraid. That's Buck Island out there. Let's go over in a couple of days. I have a golf match tomorrow. How about the day after?"

"I wish I could," Jane answered wistfully. "I have to go home that morning."

He felt as though he'd been dashed with cold water. So much for a leisurely campaign. "You can't!" he said with absolute sincerity. "There are too many things I want you to see. It's impossible."

Unhappily she pushed both hands through her blowing hair. They were getting to be very brown hands and looked nice against the soft darkness. "I can't stay. I really can't."

117

But she wanted to stay. That was obvious. *Ah,* he said to himself, *progress.*

"We'll work it out," he answered. Then he reached over, and put his own brown hand on hers, curling his fingers possessively. "In fact," he said, "I'll not let you go. There's nothing—I repeat —nothing so important as your staying here. At least through Christmas."

She said nothing more. She knew what she had to do. But it was nice to be wanted.

Feeling a bit smug that he had won, Trevor patted Jane's hand. There'd be more persuasion during the afternoon and evening. Trevor Barry was not accustomed to failure.

And if he had to move fast, well then, he would. He could count on his mother to do her part. The stage had lost a superb performer in Mother.

He turned the car in between two towering stone gateposts with carriage lanterns on the top and said, "Up ahead. That's Barry Greathouse."

The house had been planned, two hundred years ago, to make an impression, to be glimpsed in all its cool, white elegance at the end of a palm-lined lane. The palms were very old now; many had fallen like elderly giants to the inexorable crash of hurricanes, the depredations of disease and death. Their places in the row had been filled by spiked agaves, waving their creamy blossoms, by genip trees and tamarinds; still, the effect was the same—an alley of foliage, focusing the eye toward the end.

The windows of Barry Greathouse were tall and narrow, gothic, and footed with delicate grills of black wrought iron. Inside the grills, six-inch-thick oak storm shutters folded back to let in the golden sunshine. The frantic darting of little hummingbirds from red hibiscus to red hibiscus sent tiny shadows across the shallow stone steps with their curving balusters. At the top of those steps, her back to the huge black double doors, stood Naomi Barry.

Right on cue, thought Trevor, who admired his mother lavishly.

He stopped the car with a spurt of gravel, and Naomi came

down the steps, extending her hand.

"Welcome, my dears!" she said, and her voice was like velvet. "I do need reinforcements! Melissa had decided to decorate for Christmas, and it would seem her tastes run more avant-garde than mine."

Her hair was snowy and elegantly knotted in back. She smiled, exuding warmth and perfume. She swept Jane up the steps and into the black and white Empire foyer while Trevor walked behind, grinning to himself.

"Hi!" Melissa called from the top of a ladder, where she was fastening sweeping swags of some indefinable greenery. "Are you a Santa Claus person or a Christ Child person? Grandmama thinks I'm terrible, don't you, Grandmama, darling? But I find tradition just too too stagnant!"

Jane laughed. "I like tradition," she said truthfully, and was rewarded by a pat on her arm from Mrs. Barry.

"Excellent," she said. "Kindred souls, you and I. We'll leave Trevor to deal with the infant awful. There's just time to show you my house before tea. Would you like that?"

"I'd enjoy it."

Melissa giggled. "Don't show her Uncle Trev's pad," she said. "It will ruin his whole pitch."

"Shut up, brat," Trevor said cheerfully, and shook the ladder, which made her clutch and scream.

Mrs. Barry said calmly, "This way," but her eyes, upturned to her grandchild, had turned very cold.

"I am forced to admit," she went on in that beautifully articulated voice, "that I find extreme youth rather—wearing. This is our salon, my dear. The drapery was handwoven by our own people. The furniture came down from England on a frightful, stormy voyage in the late 1700's, and the Tabriz carpet my husband and I bought in an incredibly dirty souk in Cairo on our honeymoon." She sighed. "How long ago that was!"

Jane stood quite still. Ruefully she thought of the gloomy grandeur of Mrs. Van Tassel's mail-order house—Mediterranean furniture on top of wall-to-wall shag. The key to Barry Greathouse was light and air, all blue and white, with the bare

119

floors around the edge of the huge oriental rug glowing like pale honey, and coral-colored flowers seeing their mirrored reflections in polished table tops. No overstuffed chairs here; just slender, carved legs, and curved arms, ribbonbacks and French satin cushions.

"It's lovely," she said, feeling that her words were inadequate.

"We like it." Mrs. Barry smiled. "Come along."

They moved through the dining room, all gray and daffodil yellow, with an enormous, shining silver wine cooler on the sideboard and a fireplace banked with lemon leaves. They passed the study with its tooled leather paneling, and looked in at bedrooms, centered with high tester beds. Jane was almost dazed with the opulence. It was only when Mrs. Barry was called briefly to the phone that she was discerning enough to notice that some of the ceilings were water-stained and some of the drapery had been neatly mended—not only once, but again and again.

"Trevor," said his mother as they strolled back down the wide hall to the foyer, "moved into the old overseer's house some years ago. I'm a poor sleeper, and some of his friends tend to keep late hours. Come, darlings, there's tea on the terrace and I am ravenous."

What Mrs. Barry called tea was crisp, hearty salad, tiny finger sandwiches, and rich wedges of rum cake. There was also tea, in thin, ancient cups.

Mother has really pulled the stops, Trevor thought appreciatively. He sat on the low terrace wall, his white-clad legs stretched out in front of him, only half listening to his niece chatter. He was watching Jane and Naomi.

Perhaps she really likes Jane. Good. Surprisingly, so do I. How marvelous it would be if enough money to save Barry Greathouse came in a Jane package. . . .

Perhaps I ought to marry and—what's the old cliché—settle down. But Mother and I can't make it on a pittance.

I have to know how much money Jane really has. . . .

The old, standard tell-me-about-yourself-because-I-care line might do the trick. Tonight.

Jane was watching Melissa peel fruit with a pearl-handled knife. She was half smiling. Melissa glanced up and made a face.

"Well," she said a little defiantly, "Dickie didn't use his either! You know why he didn't come to the airport? His mother had him cleaning the garage and he forgot what time it was. How mundane! Oh!" she added, glancing at her watch and scrambling to her feet. "I have to get back to Limeberry. Michael's going to teach me diving."

Incredulously her uncle said, "You already know how to dive. You won the YWCA trophy three years in a row."

Melissa grinned. "Michael doesn't know that," she said. "Come on, Uncle Trev, drop me off. I want to ride in the Porsche."

Trevor nodded, rose lazily, and exchanged covert glances with his mother. He'd go; by the time he returned, Mother would have everything from Jane but her financial statement.

"Be right back," he said, and tousled Jane's head in passing. He felt exuberant confidence. This was the girl—he knew it—a good looker with money. And with that combination, marriage wouldn't be all bad.

He was gone about half an hour. On returning, his first presentiment of trouble, came when he glimpsed Jane alone on the terrace. He waved, but headed left into the cool depths of the house, where he found his mother. She was clipping flower stems with angry snaps of a shears, and the eyes she turned on him were stony.

"You absolute fool!" she said. "That girl hasn't got a dime! She's at Limeberry on one of Karen Sutton's three-dollar tour packages. You're getting old, Trevor. You're letting yourself get misled by a pretty face."

He stared at her, stunned. "But—she has a check—" he said.

"And that's all she has."

He turned to go, but she dropped the shears and grabbed his arm. "Wait, Trevor. That check. It would cover estate taxes. Get it."

"You're crazy. I—" Then he stopped, worried. There wasn't anyone else. There could be possible prey on the cruise boats, but

121

establishing contacts took a long time—and he hadn't even tried. He'd been so sure of Jane. A little flame of anger curled up in him. How dare she deceive Trevor Barry!

"All right," he said briefly. "I'll see what I can do."

"Don't see! Do!"

"How do you propose—"

"I don't. That's your business."

She turned her back to him and began snipping stems again.

He stared at her rigid shoulders a moment, jingling the change in his pockets, suddenly feeling very tired and very old. "All right. I'll bring her back here tonight. Tell the help to stay away."

"Nothing messy. Remember Melissa."

"You worry about Melissa. I'll need gas."

She cursed; it was always a shock to him, coming from that patrician mouth. "Why can't you conduct your seductions in a Ford like everybody else!"

"You didn't bring me up to appreciate Fords, Mother dearest." He was holding out his hand.

She shrugged, dug into a linen pocket, and put money in his hand. "I hope they picked her clean in the shops," she said.

"We did all right."

He went back to the door, but stood in the cool shadows a moment, looking out at Jane in the sunshine.

He felt a little sick. She was a sweet kid, and she had a delicious body. Was there any possible way to work without hurting her?

He'd try making love first, with music, wine, furs, and soft touches. If that didn't work, well, there were always the cameras. And the people back home. Howard, perhaps. Blackmail was dirty, but it usually worked.

CHAPTER XI

Trevor took Jane back to Limeberry the long way around the island. Once, on a rare straight stretch, he suddenly accelerated and drove very fast. Jane was a bit scared as the trees flashed by in blurs and her eyes stung. But as abruptly as he'd speeded up he slowed down, and putting out one brown hand, he patted one of hers.

Jane took a deep breath. "I guess I'm chicken," she said.

He grinned that flash of white teeth in a brown face she was growing to know well. "I wish I were," he answered.

They turned into the white-graveled drive at Limeberry. He let her out under the tamarind trees.

"It's been a lovely day," Jane said, "even if you do drive too fast on the wrong side of the road."

"My darling, the day is not over. I shall return in half an hour in my best dinner clothes. Put on your most beguiling gown, for we dine with the poshest tonight."

He was half turned toward her open door, his arm laying along the back of the seat. The golden sun came through the gnarled old tree branches in moving stripes, touching the silver in his hair, the flat chest and stomach muscles outlined clearly through the thin shirt.

Why did she suddenly think of tigers ready to spring? She hesitated. "Oh, thank you, but I—"

Then, beyond him, in the arcade, she saw Tom Nelson. His back was to them, and it was quite a way across the lawn; nonetheless, she saw him distinctly. Marlene Von Fox was in his arms—Marlene, either in her black bikini or absolutely nothing. As Jane stared, Marlene's long-fingered hands crept up to the back of Tom's dark head, and bent it down toward hers.

"All right," Jane said to Trevor Barry. "Thank you very much. I'll be ready."

As she ran up the cool stairs to her room, she was shocked—

both at the tumult in her chest the sight of Tom and Marlene had caused, and at the anger, the unreasonable, unexplainable anger—that was boiling up from her toes to her head.

She flung herself into the shower, dried off, brushed her hair, scrubbed her teeth, did her face. Then she put perfume in all the proper places.

The strapless bra had left angry red marks on her white body. She put it on again, wincing, slipped into her beautiful long white dress, and stared at herself in the mirror.

The bra hurt and its lines showed through on the dress.

She slowly slipped down the tiny straps of the dress, took off the bra, flung it into a corner, and slipped the straps back up again, settling her bare breasts in their soft, silky pockets.

No one cared what she did! No one!

And the dress looked fantastic. *She* looked fantastic.

"The hell with everything!" said Jane. She picked up her crystalline clutch bag and went downstairs.

Karen had glimpsed Jane's return. Leaving her small son happily splashing in his tub, she was just coming along the passage to see if Jane was staying for dinner when she saw her coming down the stairs.

The knife-pleated, nightgownlike dress flowed behind Jane beautifully, but her breasts bobbed with each step and it was obvious that they were quite unencumbered. Her makeup was much heavier than usual too. And beneath it Jane's face was set, her eyes smoldering.

She saw Karen. With an effort at lightness she said, "I won't be in to dinner. I was going to tell you. I'm going out."

"With Trevor?" It was none of Karen's business, absolutely none of her business, but she had to ask.

"Yes."

Karen put out a helpless hand, and touched Jane's bare shoulder. "Oh, my dear," she said with great concern, "do be careful."

"Why?" asked Jane between her teeth as she went out the door.

Standing stock still in the cool hallway, Karen heard Trevor's voice, a car door, and the sound of the Porsche spinning gravel as it pulled away. This time she didn't linger to wonder where on the island Trev had credit enough to get his hands on a Porsche. That was now a very unimportant item. Suddenly Karen was scared.

She turned, and sped back along the hallway. Tom was just coming out of the laundry room, where Addie had pressed his suit for the funeral tomorrow. She grabbed him, and he grabbed her to keep her from falling. "Whoa, settle down," he said. He shifted the suit, leaned against the cool stone wall and listened—first seriously, then with anger of his own.

"It's none of our business," he said harshly.

"Tom, she's an infant!"

"Infant!" he repeated, and laughed. It was not a nice laugh. "Sure she is—like I'm Howdy Doody! Cool it, Karen. If she'd decided to hand it out, I'm sure Trevor is accepting and it's certainly no damned affair of ours! She can take care of herself—believe me she can!" His free hand went to the hard line of his jaw reminiscently.

Karen was staring. "Who are you talking about?"

"Who are *you* talking about? Crystal Bell!"

"Crystal Bell! You ninny! You idiot! Who do you think you just put to bed, boiled as a barn owl? Marlene Von Fox—*that's* Crystal Bell!"

It was his turn to stare. Furiously she poked a finger in his face. "Von Fox was her last husband's name—or the first husband—I don't remember. I don't care! I do care about that . . . that baby who just walked out of here half naked with the most depraved lecher on the island! Because she can't take care of herself! And we have to do something!"

She saw her brother whiten beneath his tan. "Oh, my God," he said softly.

What a colossal bonehead he was! *He'd* made the mistake in the motel—*he'd* made the mistake this morning! Now the shock on her face made sense, and it was like a knife in him.

It was his turn to grab his sister's arm. Hoarsely he asked, "Where did they go?"

"I don't know! She was dressed foolishly! Oh, that poor

blessed child. She has no idea what she's in for with Trev, but she did look smashing. Where would he take her to show off?"

He said it through his teeth: "That damned pit of his in the overseer's house—behind Naomi's."

"Not first! They'll dine somewhere. Where does Trev still have credit?"

He frowned, trying to think.

"The Trevanyan!" she said. "He shills for them with the tour ships. They'll let him in."

"That's it. Let's go."

She grabbed him. "Tom, we can't just go barging in there."

He stopped, and glared down at her, his dark brows a bar of anger in his tanned face. "What then?"

"I'll tell Addie to serve the guests. Jump into your dinner clothes; thank God they came back from the cleaner's yesterday. I'll throw on something. We'll go into the Trevanyan like any other couple."

"What then?"

"I don't know—we'll think of that on the way."

He slapped her on the fanny. "Go!"

Unfortunately halfway to Frederiksted the old bus had a flat. Karen sat inside, chewing a nail in fierce concentration while Tom rolled out the spare. It was an efficient operation; nonetheless, they lost half an hour. Pulling his coat back on, he slid in beside her and started the engine.

"You have a smudge," she said, dabbing at his cheek. "What are we going to say: My, what a surprise, and may we dine with you?"

He pulled the bus onto the island road just as the sun slid out of sight, leaving them in a world of half shadows. Grimly, Tom answered his sister, "Trev knows us better than that."

"He also knows we don't dine at the Trevanyan. But we certainly can't just dash in and say, Unhand this innocent female!"

"I can," said Tom shortly. His mouth was set in an ominous line.

"Tom, you can't! Making Trev angry is one thing, but humiliating him is another. In front of other people, I mean. We'll just have to play it by ear."

Tom knew which ear he would play it by. Trevor's. Karen had told him the rest of what she knew about Jane as they rode along, and he was kicking himself.

How much did he care about her? He didn't know. How much could you care about a girl you'd met six days ago? Enough. A good start.

He found a parking place among the fancier cars in the Trevanyan lot, helped Karen out, and they went up the shallow stone steps to the double doors. The Trevanyan was a converted town house. The decor was opulently French. By a Louis Quintze console with elaborate, gilded dolphins, the headwaiter looked at them dubiously. The lapels of Tom's dinner coat were a bit wide for this year's fashion. The waiter wasn't quite sure about a table.

"We'll sit at the bar," said Tom flatly, and towed his sister away by her wrist.

"We'll never get a table!" she whispered.

"Stick their tables! We're here to find Jane. One scotch on the rocks and a vodka martini."

"Very dry," said Karen automatically. She wriggled up on a stool beside Tom, and scanned the crowded dance floor. "Tom, there they are."

"Where?"

"There."

In a sea of white dinner coats and whiter mess jackets, Trevor and Jane were dancing slowly. Jane was close to Trevor, very close. *The old goat,* Karen thought nastily. Just then Trevor looked up and saw Karen. He looked surprised—and not pleasantly so.

He knows we can't afford the Trevanyan, Karen realized. *He's wondering now why we are here. Oh, dear . . .*

The kaleidoscope of the dancers shifted again, and the pair was gone. Karen kept watching, but she didn't see them again. Tom had turned back to the bar and was scribbling a note on a cocktail napkin. Some folding money changed hands and one of the bartenders disappeared.

"What did you say?" Karen asked.

"I said to give it to the lady with Mr. Barry," he answered.

"In the note! The note!"

"I asked her to meet you in the john."

"Oh! Then I'd better go."

She slid off the stool and disappeared into the crowd. Tom tasted his scotch, decided he didn't want it, and pushed the glass away. The bartender came back.

"I'm sorry, sir. Mr. Barry and his party have dined and gone."

Tom slid off his stool, shelling out more bills. Damn. Now how was he going to get Karen out of the john?

A large sunburned lady in a small dress was the answer. "Sure, fella," she said. "Green dress."

"Right."

He waited impatiently, smoked his first cigarette in weeks, and stubbed it out half smoked in a potted asparagus fern.

Karen reappeared. She was almost smiling. "You know, of course, that woman thought I was anything but your sister."

He shrugged. Other people's thoughts weren't his problem. "They've gone."

"Where?"

"God knows. It's early. You know, sis, this is pretty awkward."

"I do know." They looked at each other miserably.

"I feel responsible for her," Karen said.

Tom didn't say what he felt, only, "Well, let's go looking."

They did look, spending much more money than they could afford. They found nothing, which was really more ominous than if they were on the trail but two steps behind.

In another parking lot Tom tapped the steering wheel with hard fingers. "I'm simple," he said harshly. "I'm naive and stupid and dumb. That bartender lied. They were still there."

Karen sighed and nodded. "Perhaps. Trev did see us. That alarms me even more—that he'd try to shake us, I mean. And, of course, they wouldn't be there now."

"No."

"So where?"

He looked at his watch, tilting his arm in the moonlight. "Barry Greathouse."

"Oh, Tom . . ."

He put the bus in gear and backed out. Worried, Karen asked, "Tom, what shall we do when we get there?"

He shook his dark head. "I haven't the slightest," he said, and headed the bus up the street. "You do realize," he added, "that we may end up looking like two clowns."

"I know. But—that girl—I just can't take a chance, Tom."

He touched her hand lightly. "I know, Carrot," he said. "Neither can I."

"I just have to be sure she's all right. What she wants to do is her affair."

His only reply was to turn onto Centerline Road and head through the limpid moonlight for Barry Greathouse.

Six champagne cocktails previously, Jane Doorn was doing the same thing. She leaned back against the seat of the Porsche, letting her hair flow in the warm, scented night air, and examined her feelings. She felt strange—as though there were bubbles inside her. She put her hand to her nose and stuck a finger in her eye by mistake. "Trev," she said. "Am I drunk?"

He laughed, a deep chuckle in his chest, and took one hand from the wheel to sweep her over against his warm chest. "Not really," he said. "And the fresh air will take care of it, anyway."

"Where are we going?"

"Home. My home, I mean. Mother showed you her house. I'll show you mine. Fair enough?"

"Fair enough." There had been something strange said about Trev's house, but it eluded her.

He turned on the radio. The soft music added to the spicy warm scent of tamarinds, the vanilla of the oleanders, the faint, abrasive tang of salt. Trevor leaned his cheek against Jane's head, and was rubbing it gently with his jaw. She was certainly a gorgeous armful. And she had the check! He'd seen it in her clutch purse as she'd taken out a lipstick. Things were going his way.

He turned off short of the gateposts, and drove down a smooth lane behind a barrier hedge. His house was small, hip-roofed, and gleamed white in the moonlight. He got out and held out his hand to Jane. She slid out obediently, started to stand, caught her heel and pitched forward into his arms. He kissed her for the first time—a gentle, exploratory kiss, tracing the shape of her mouth with his tongue. She drew back and looked up at him a little startled.

So. Midwestern provincial are we, he thought. *All right. No sweat. We'll just progress by stages. . . .*

He grinned. "Welcome to Barry Smallhouse," he said and walked her up the shallow steps.

He'd said her legs would obey her. They wouldn't. She still felt the bubbles, as though she were moving six inches above the ground. It worried her. She was alone, drunk, and going into a man's house in the middle of the night.

Well, Jane, you wanted a big adventure! Your candle is burning at both ends now. See if you like the light. . . .

"Stand still," he said. "I'll turn on a lamp in a moment. I want to touch a match to the fire."

She leaned against a wall that felt silky, and listened to him going surefooted across the room in the dark. *But it's his house,* she thought. *Of course he can move in the dark. Like a cat. Like a tiger.*

There was a scratching sound, and a bright amber flame shot up. She saw a cavernous stone fireplace on the other side of a huge, long couch. In it the fire began to lick yellow and red, casting flickering shadows over the room. Trev came back to her and, without speaking, knelt and took off her shoes. She saw that his were already off and sitting by the door.

"I spent a great deal of money on this carpet," he said, laughing, "and people cannot enjoy it in shoes."

"Oh! It's like velvet!" she said.

"Nice, right? Curl up on the couch, darling. I'll get us something to drink."

What was the speech, she wondered. *I really should be going? That was it. That was the speech all right.*

She walked across the deep, sensuous velvet and sat on the couch before the leaping flames. Soft music came from all around, punctuated by the sharp click of ice and the sounds of a shaker. She had a sense of unreality, heightened by the champagne.

This is not me. Not really. If it is, I'll wake up. I don't do these things. . . .

"Here you are, my love."

He was bending over her, offering her a stemmed glass. He'd taken off his coat and tie and unbuttoned the ruffled shirt front. A thin, gold chain dangled from his throat as he bent, and the fire made little pinpoints of light dance in his eyes.

She took the glass. He had one of his own. He sat down beside her—close beside her. They both stretched their feet to the flames.

"Sip," he said. "I pride myself on a superb martini."

After the first taste of vaguely oily cold, it wasn't bad. She sipped. He stirred and put his arm around her again.

"Nice," he said. "Much better than the hullabaloo in the bistros."

The fire crackled. They sipped.

"What is the cover on this couch?" she asked.

"Fur—and you don't want to know. It's an endangered species. Drink up a little. Martinis are not good when warm."

"Trev, are you trying to get me drunk?"

"My love, I don't seem to have to try. But, no, I'm not. I don't like making love with someone who is slopped. The subtleties get lost."

She turned her head, tried to look up at him and the movement made her a little dizzy. She put the martini down. "Who said we were going to—to make love?"

"Did anyone have to say it?"

"That's a subtlety?"

"That's a subtlety."

He refilled his glass. She put her hand on top of his and said, "No."

He shrugged. A golden ripple from muted harps poured into the air from the hidden stereo. *Right on cue,* he thought complacently, and kissed her lightly on one cheek, sliding his lips down to nibble the tip of an ear. His lips were cold from the martini. "You have a divine smell," he said.

A small pulse had started beating in her throat. It was saying, *I'm not sure I want to be here.*

She started to move away, but he murmured, "Don't do that." He stretched lazily, putting down his glass. With the tip of his finger he began to trace the shape of her eyes, the length of her nose, the oval of her mouth, kissing each lightly in turn, saying against her mouth, "Such a lovely dress, but God, the lovelier things inside it . . ." His finger slid down her throat, and a hand gently pushed down the slim white straps of her dress. Her own hands came out, but whether to push or cling she wasn't sure. His breath came fast, hard, and warm; it mixed with the alcohol in her brain to form a hazy need to move closer, to seek the smooth stroke of his fingers as he slowly cupped her breasts, drawing them free of the dress, holding them up to his urgent, searching mouth. "All evening," he whispered into the sweet valley between them, "all evening they've been saying, Kiss me, kiss me, and I've been promising, I will, I will." His other arm went down her back, arching it firmly, almost sliding her beneath him. Her head spun mistily. She wanted—she wanted. What was happening to her body? What did she want? Then his hot mouth began to kiss her tingling breasts and she flushed scarlet at the intimacy of his touch. This wasn't what she wanted. Not this blind, lust-filled groping. Not these kisses from a man she hardly knew, one she didn't quite trust.

Suddenly all drunken pleasure fled. Almost sober with self-reproach, she tried to pull away, but found herself rigidly trapped by his body half on top of hers. "Stop!" she whispered hoarsely. "Stop it!"

"Oh, you want to play rough, do you," he said. "I like a little resistance myself. It makes surrender so much sweeter." His weight shifted to bring him into even closer contact. He was crushing her, hurting her.

His body pressing down on her and something in the sound of his voice struck terror like a shaft in her heart. She began to struggle. Snarling like an animal, he pinned her down, fighting her.

Then she screamed.

Tom and Karen had been sitting outside for fifteen minutes, sunk in misery and embarrassment. But when Jane screamed there was no longer any question. Tom was up the steps in a leap, his shoulder to the door. He charged into the firelit room, for a moment seeing no one. Then Trevor's head appeared over the back of the couch. His hair was in his eyes, and his eyes were black with passion and anger. "What the hell—"

Tom hit him squarely on the jaw. His fist made a satisfying crack. Trev fell backward, scrambling with his hands. From around the end of the couch came a white ghost, flying into Karen's arms.

"Get her out of here," Tom said hoarsely. He was panting with anger and exertion. His fists doubled, he waited.

Slowly Trev hoisted himself to his feet, and braced himself against the stone fireplace. He was holding his jaw with his hand. "Get off my rug!" he said in a thick voice. "Get off my rug with your dirty shoes!"

In a succinct voice Tom told him where to put his rug. Then he turned and left.

CHAPTER XII

On the way back to Limeberry, Jane sat between Karen and Tom. Jane was a shivering, snuffling bundle wrapped in a blanket close in the circle of Karen's protective arm. Tom, keeping both hands on the wheel, was taking great satisfaction in a set of bleeding knuckles. Karen made soothing noises, and Jane kept saying, in a mixture of relief and shame, "Thank you—thank you—I was so scared."

Once she sat upright, clutched Tom's arm in a sort of agony, and asked, "Tom, did he hurt you?"

"Never laid a finger on me," he answered and grinned. "It's all right, kid. It's all right."

Dumb as it might be, he felt good. Jane was okay.

In a small voice she was saying, "May I have another Kleenex?"

Karen found the box empty. Jane said, "There's some in my bag, oh, my bag—"

"I have it." On the run back into the house Karen had grabbed it up. Now she leaned forward, snapped on the map light, and undid the clasp.

She knew about the check Jane was carrying; Jane had told her. But when she saw the name, McIlhenny and McIlhenny, she frowned. There was something strange here. McIlhenny and McIlhenny, as she knew very well, were not insurance brokers. Not by any means.

Putting that item aside to tell Tom later, she found the Kleenex, tucked it into Jane's moist little fist, and closed the purse.

Jane blew mightily.

Tom chuckled as he turned into the Limeberry drive. "Good God," he said. "What do we need with hurricanes?" He felt good. It was ridiculous, but true.

He climbed out, went around, and opened the door for the women. Clutching her blanket, Jane stepped down behind Karen, wobbled on the hard, crushed shell of the drive, and said, "My shoes!"

"Never mind," she added grimly. "I don't think I ever want to see them again."

"I'll go up with you," Karen said.

"No, I'm all right. I just don't know how to thank you—"

"Courtesy of the house," Karen answered.

Jane smiled a rather pitiful smile in return, made a sort of half gesture toward Tom, then turned and started up the stairs.

"Carrot, after the funeral tomorrow," Tom asked quietly, "may I have the rest of the day off?"

"I don't see why not."

He nodded and went to the foot of the stairs. "Jane."

She turned, presenting such a woebegone face that it wrung his heart.

"Grandmama Louise's funeral is tomorrow morning," he said. "I should be free about eleven. May I show you Fredriksted—not the one you've seen, but the real one?"

One hand clutched her blanket. The other clung to the railing, and he saw the knuckles whiten. A little stiffly, almost whispering, she said, "Please, don't be kind to me."

"Goddamnit," he answered rudely, "don't you think that's my decision? Will you go, or won't you?"

"I will. Yes."

"Good girl," he said.

A shaft of light from the top of the stairwell caught his face as he looked up. His tie was awry, he was beginning to need a shave, and his eyes were mere black caverns beneath heavy dark brows, but he was smiling.

"Good night too," he said. He patted her hand, turned, and went on down the hall.

In her cool, white room, Jane dropped the blanket, and for a long time just lay in a silent heap across the blue bed. The soft drapes of her dress stirred in the light breeze through the louvered balcony doors, bringing the now familiar scent of vanilla, and the whish-whishing sound of the incessant sea upon the shore.

At last she got up and took off her dress. Almost naked in the half-light, she looked at the dress with loathing, thinking fiercely, *I'm going to throw it away. I can never wear it again.*

But common sense told her, *You can't throw it away. You have too much money tied up in it. And perhaps seeing it will remind you to use a little more judgment—something you've exhibited none of so far.*

She went to the bathroom to take off her makeup, and for the first time looked at herself—and was sick at the sight of the smudged, garish travesty of a face that looked back.

My God, she thought, *it can't be me! That's a—a—* (and she finally dredged up one of her mother's favorite words) *a hussy! Cheap and tattered and used. That's me.*

In anguish she realized why Tom Nelson was taking her out tomorrow. It was her last day, and he felt sorry for her. Or he didn't want her giving Limeberry Vacations a bad name.

But I don't care, she thought defiantly, and her chin went up. *It is my last day of vacation. And I'm going to go!*

She did not sleep well. In fact, she scarcely slept at all. She had had an experience totally beyond her wildest imagining. It had left her sick and shaken.

I wanted adventure, she thought with self-disgust. *I wanted excitement to remember all the rest of my life. Well, I've had it. And I will remember. How can I ever forget?*

She thought of Howard and went cold all over. Would he be like that—like Trevor Barry—suddenly not a human being at all?

She didn't know. She couldn't know, and she put her hands to her face, moaning with revulsion. There was no one to ask, no one to talk to.

When morning sent its pale gray bars in through the louvered door, she went to sleep, restless at first, sighing a little. At ten she was wakened by the soft, faraway sound of singing.

For a moment she lay perfectly still, staring at the ceiling. What had wakened her?

Then the sound came again. It was a blend of voices on the translucent, shimmering warm air—voices half chanting, with

137

now and then a "Yes, Lord!" and "Hallelujah!" coming in like a thin rich thread of color woven through a simple design.

Jane threw off the sheets, pulled on her robe and, with it belling behind her like a sail, she went out on the balcony.

Then she understood. Grandmama Louise's children were taking her to her last resting place.

An old pick-up truck, battered but polished and waxed, waited at the far gate. Its bed was carefully covered with a white sheet fastened with bright ribbons. Knots of long gladiola fanned along the sides, their multiple blossoms still freshly pink in the cool morning air. From the arcade came a slow procession headed by the gray-haired pastor.

Six men carried the plain black coffin. They were buttoned into sober suits, all taken from some dim corner of unused closets and already showing damp patches of sweat between the shoulderblades. Behind the coffin walked Addie, solidly corsetted into a prim Sunday dress, her tear-streaked face shaded by the brim of an enormous flowered hat. With her was Nat, in rusty black; it was his rich baritone that led the voices. Behind them in a diminishing tail came the rest of the clan, including children, who were subdued in too-short long pants, the little girls wearing thin bright Easter dresses. Last came Karen and Tom. Karen's white skirt fluttered in the morning air, and Tom, in coat and tie, carried little Tod on one arm. They were all singing, and the sound tore at Jane's already battered heart.

She watched while they slid the coffin into the truck. It lurched and went slowly out the gate. The procession followed. Some of the children, she noticed, were tightly gripping small white prayer books.

How different, she thought grimly, from her own mother's funeral. She went back inside, remembering the cold, damp church, the staring eyes, the dull, monotonous, mundane words spoken indifferently over a bronze casket she could ill afford. Howard had said it was expected of her. And the flowers—stiff, wired sticks with blossoms already browning.

The scene outside her window just then had conveyed a sense

of loss—but also there'd been air, sunshine, and fresh country flowers and singing.

Poor Mother, she thought. But the grief was gone. The memories that were left were now blurring at the edges, the querulous, suspicious voice softening in retrospect. She only clearly remembered her mother's years of pain and was glad, once more, that the suffering was over.

But remembering Mother brought inevitably another thought to her mind. What would Mother say about her only daughter now?

I can't think about it! I won't think about it! Nor about Howard —nor anything at home!

This is my last day and I will not have it ruined!

Remembering how she had looked last night revolted her, so she barely put on lipstick let alone other makeup. *Shorts,* she thought, *and that loose cotton shirt. I'll not have Tom Nelson think I'm trying to seduce him. I'll try to be calm and matter-of-fact. Impersonal. Pleasant, of course. But he has to know I understand he's just being nice to a guest!*

She stuffed essentials back into her big canvas shoulder bag and started out the door, almost falling over last evening's shoes, which had been left in the hallway. As she recognized them, her heart shot into her throat.

Gingerly she picked them up by their straps, tossed them back inside behind her, and shut the door. Despite her fervent hope never to see him again, Trevor Barry came into view as she descended the stairs. He was shaven, brushed, and dressed in a trim polo shirt and slacks. Marlene Von Fox, in a clinging halter dress, was on his arm. While they passed beneath her, he was saying, "I hope you brought lots of money, love. I have friends in all the shops."

"Lots, darling," said Marlene in her throaty, curiously thickened voice. "Lots of lovely, lovely money to spend on you, if you're good."

They stopped beneath Jane and kissed. It was an explicit embrace, leaving no questions as to their relationship. As Marlene broke away, laughing like a satisfied tabby cat, Trevor glanced up, and saw Jane.

He grimaced. That was all. Then he walked out of the house arm in arm with Ms. Von Fox.

Left to herself Jane let out a lungful of pent-up breath. Then she went down for coffee, and sat under the tamarind trees with Mr. Davis to wait for Tom.

"It's snowing in Quincy," Mr. Davis announced with a sort of gloomy relish. He was reclining on a lawn chair in new shorts and regarding his bright red knees with rueful pleasure. "I meant to get me a dandy tan to show the boys, but if I sit out in the sun any more I believe I'll blister." He cast an approving eye at Jane. "Now, yours is coming along real nice. You brown easy. Like Madge. Isn't it a shame how quick it'll fade when we get back?"

Jane nodded. She moved her chair to the sun, stretched her legs out straight, and closed her eyes.

"I saw that Barry fellow just leave with Ms. Von Fox," he went on chattily. "If he knows what's good for him, he'll keep that lady away from the beer joints."

Jane's eyes popped open. "Why?"

"Lord, child, she's a lush. Haven't you noticed? Poor Tom. He had a terrible time getting loose from her yesterday. When she's drunk, she gets sort of—you know—" His face reddened suddenly, realizing he'd let his conversation reach an awkward place.

"Like a cat in heat," said his wife crisply. She appeared in a long beach robe, loaded with cameras, pillows, lotion, and knitting. "Come along, Willard. This is our last day by the sea and I want you to take a lot of pictures. Did he tell you it was snowing in Quincy, dear? Brrrr. I suppose it will be a blizzard when we get there."

"Probably," said Jane. Despite her resolutions, she shivered. The idea of going back made her cold all over.

Willard stood up, grinning a sly grin. "Madge got her bee-kini," he said, and suddenly lifted a corner of his wife's robe. She squealed and slapped his hand.

140

"Doesn't look too bad," he said, "for an old lady."

"Willard Davis," she snapped, "you are a dirty old man!"

But she was laughing. "It's not a bikini, either," she said to Jane. "I've sense enough to know that skimpy bathing suits don't go with orthopedic shoes. Are you going into town, dear?"

"Yes. With Tom."

After she said it, she blushed.

"He's a nice young man," said Mrs. Davis maternally. "No remarks, Willard," she added, and took her grinning husband down the path to the beach.

Someone had left a jaunty straw hat on the lawn table. Jane picked it up and fanned her hot face. *Now why did I have to mention Tom,* she asked herself. *Dumb. Dumb!*

She closed her eyes again against the sun, and dropped off to sleep.

A few moments later Tom Nelson came striding up the path from his windmill, turned left, and went through the hedge to the front lawn. He was wearing jeans and a blue chambray shirt. His hair was still wet and curled around his ears. He was whistling between his teeth—not happily, but reflectively. Karen had told him about the McIlhenny check; it was apparent that someone was taking Jane for a ride. Who, he didn't know—nor even if it was any of his business. That must remain to be seen.

He stopped short upon seeing Jane. He was becoming familiar with the feeling that always washed over him in her presence. He'd always wanted her—but now he felt tenderness as well. And a little hope.

He could almost feel sorry for Trevor. The man was fighting a losing battle against himself, and against his mother, with Barry Greathouse strapped on his back. They'd probably find him dead someday in that velvety passion pit of his. Would those hidden cameras designed to catch rich ladies in compromising situations catch some rich husband slitting Trevor's throat?

And had that been it with Jane? Had Trevor thought her rich? *Why not,* Tom admitted wryly, *I did.*

He bent and touched Jane's shoulder. It was warm with sun,

and smooth to his fingers. "Hey, there, sleeping beauty. Ready to go visit the big town?"

Her eyes opened, amber with sleep. For a moment she stared. In that one moment Tom saw something in those eyes for him, for him alone.

Then she blinked, smiled, and stretched. "Have I kept you waiting?"

"Not at all. I just got changed. I'm glad you brought a hat; the sun is going to be a scorcher today."

"I didn't. I mean—it's not mine."

He picked it up and glanced inside. "It's my sister's. Take it anyway. She won't mind." He put out a brown hand and pulled her upright. "Let's move. Karen wants us back for a cookout tonight."

A small finger of disappointment touched Jane. She realized in dismay how much she'd counted on having Tom all to herself all day. But she smiled, picked up the hat and the bag, and followed him through the barrier hedge to the bus.

It stood patiently beneath genip trees, buzzing with fat bees staggering from blossom to blossom. Tom got in, pulled Jane up, and started the engine. A frantic "Hey!" made them both turn. Melissa came running across the lawn. She had a red hibiscus behind one ear and looked smashingly pretty in very brief shorts. She hauled herself on board, panting. "Drop me at Grand-mama's, will you, Tom? I've got to tell her I'm not staying for Christmas. I can't bear to have Michael go tomorrow without me. We may get married in Quincy."

Tom strictly obeyed the first sentence. He'd heard Jane's little indrawn breath. "I'll drop you at the end of the lane, okay? And your return is on your own."

"Oh, that's all right. Grandmama said I could drive the Cor-niche if I bought gas." She plopped herself behind Jane. "I'm seventeen—that's old enough to get married, isn't it? And Mi-chael's a tech—something—anyway, he's in line for another stripe; then he could live off base and I could live with him. Besides, he thinks he's going to Germany, and wouldn't that be neat? I've always wanted to live abroad. I used to go with a guy

142

named Greg. He was going to be a tennis star and play at Wimbleton, which would be pretty nifty too, except then I met Dick. Besides, Grandmama hasn't been much fun this time. She and Uncle Trev have flaming rows and then he looks so crushed. Are you going on into Frederiksted? I want some boiled peanuts and Grandmama thinks they are too plebian."

The chatter went on nonstop until she hopped off at the stone gateposts and went dancing happily up the alley of palms and agave. Tom puffed his cheeks and blew out expressively.

"No more passengers," he said. "Michael must have iron ears. But Karen will be glad she is going home. Naomi has given her no supervision whatsoever, and it's rather been a bad scene all around."

He turned off Centerline into a small side road that wound between palm trees, spiky century plants, and a scattering of small tin-roofed houses hung with Ginger Thomas vines. Several children, casually clad, crouched together in the tough grass. Lean dogs yawned from deep shadows. As they maneuvered around a rattling two-wheeled wooden cart pulled in a desultory fashion by an indifferent horse and driven by a nodding gentleman in a large straw hat, Jane suddenly realized they'd been in Frederiksted for some time. The houses were closer together now, two-storied. There were deep stone arcades fronting the street, arcades whose cool depth the hot sun never touched, and high, wooden galleries encircling tin roofs and heavy shutters, so burdened with fancy gingerbread that they almost seemed hung with ancient lace. And everywhere there were gates—gates leading into gardens, gates barring the way through slits between buildings, allowing a glimpse of greenery beyond, gates behind which old stairs climbed into ornate cupolas, gates that banned the passersby from narrow walkways flanked by cactus planted in coy Victorian flowerboxes.

Tom turned the corner, barely missing a casual stack of barrels and parked in front of a long, tattered, balconied building labeled in faded letters, RUSTOLI'S EMPORIUM. Nests of merchandise spilled out haphazardly onto the hot sidewalk. Brooms, baskets, and cases of powdered milk provided scanty shade for the lank dogs drowsing in the sunshine.

Tom swung out and said, "Be just a minute." Jane idly watched his long legs striding into the shadows, then turned her attention to the people on the street. She saw large, shapeless ladies in large, shapeless dresses, tall gaunt ladies in crisp aprons like Addie's, with shoulder ruffles so big and starched, it almost seemed they could fly. Feet slap-slapped in loose, formless shoes, and on top of bright head scarves sat large straw hats. On top of the hats were balanced incredible burdens like shoe boxes and potted plants—all riding perfectly smoothly, without a wobble.

When Tom suddenly appeared before Jane, she cried, "That woman has a birdcage on her head!"

Tom grinned. "Or a washtub or a sack of groceries or a jar of peanut butter," he said. "It leaves your hands free for more important things. Come on. We can leave the bus and walk from here."

He helped her down, then reached into his hip pocket and produced a folded, faded golf hat. "There," he said, fitting it neatly above his eyes. "Let's go down on the strand. The air is cooler off the water, and maybe we can find the ice cream man."

They did find him. From hand-cranked freezers in the trunk of his rusting Plymouth, he dipped ice cream into Dixie Cups, putting the money neatly into a cupcake pan. Eating the lovely, sweet coolness with blue plastic spoons, Tom and Jane walked slowly along the seawall, admiring the faded, weatherbeaten gentility of the old Victorian houses in view. A lean, sleepy dog padded silently behind them, patiently waiting. At last, unable to stand it any longer, Jane knelt, and let him shove both nose and pink tongue deep into her cup, savoring the final elusive taste.

Tom took both cups, crumpled them, and tossed the balls into a barrel. "Too hot?" he asked.

"Oh, no. Not yet. What's down there?"

"A marina. Can you row a boat?"

"I'll never admit it."

He laughed and turned instead up the street into the languid

144

laughter and chatter of a market place. Exotic heaps of melons and grapes flanked trays of emerald peppers, flaming mangos, and bouquets of asparagus. Squawking chickens shied at tubs of flaccid fish. Through it all slapped the shifting, chattering kaleidoscope of cheerful vendors, careful buyers, traders, and a few camera-hung tourists.

"Not many tourists find their way here," Tom said. He handed a dark man with an elaborate straw hat a few coins, dipped into a cool tub and came up with two dripping cans of Coke. "Dry work," he said, "escorting an outlander," and grinned. They found a vacant palm tree and sat beneath it, sipping their drinks. Inevitably Jane remembered yesterday and the immaculate man in white slacks across the table from her in that expensive yacht club. She looked at Tom, dressed in jeans, his brown arms on his knees, his feet in tennis shoes, totally relaxed beneath a scruffy palm tree. From the brim of that shapeless golf hat she found him looking at her.

"Is it all right?" he asked softly. "Would you like to go somewhere else?"

"Oh, no," she said. "Nowhere in the world." Then she took a deep breath and tried to smile. "I hate to think of going home tomorrow, that's all."

His eyes hadn't wavered. "Do you have to go?"

What other answer was there? She knew she had to go back. She'd always known. "Yes," she answered soberly. "I do. You can only run so far."

"What were you running from?"

"From myself, mostly," she answered painfully. "From the person I was."

"And aren't now?"

"Oh, I suppose I am . . . beneath the varnish and veneer. People don't really change, I guess."

He drained his soda can, and put it carefully between his feet. "What do you do—back there?"

"I keep books. In an electronics shop."

"Do you like it?"

"I—I don't know. It's the only job I've ever had." She turned

145

her own can in her hands, drawing designs in the beaded moisture with one finger. "My mother was sick for a long time. I just stayed home and looked after her. And went to work, of course." She looked up and tried to smile. "I'm afraid I'm not very exciting."

"Look, kid," he said, "if I wanted entertainment, I'd go to a movie. Your father is dead too?"

"Yes."

"No brothers or sisters?"

"No."

"Then why go back?"

She took a deep breath. He knew something was coming, and he desperately wished he hadn't asked the question—not yet, not so early in the day.

"I'm supposed to get married," she said hopelessly. "Right after Christmas. To a very nice man."

There it was. Yet something was not right. "*Is* he nice?" he asked very quietly.

She fell into the trap. "Yes. Everyone says so."

"Do you say so?"

She couldn't meet his eyes. She kept turning the can in her fingers, turning and turning. "Yes," she answered. "I—I guess he is."

"You guess!" His deep voice was still quiet, but it came to her ears like thunder. "That's a hell of a poor answer, woman! Don't you *know*?"

The can crackled under her grip. The words burst from her: "I promised!"

There was the nitty-gritty. She had promised.

He plucked a long blade of grass, and tied it in knots, spacing each one carefully. "Tell me about this guy."

Not even those words came easy, but they built a picture. Howard was a turkey—a first class s.o.b. But he offered all those things a mamma thinks her little daughter should have and this Jane was a mamma's girl. The mother was dead, but she still had her grip on Jane.

"What does this paragon do besides spread virtue?"

She looked up at him, and the expression in her eyes hurt him clear to his tennis shoes. Quietly he amended his words.

"What does he do for a living?"

"He's a banker."

Bingo! The McIlhenny check in mind, he asked, "I suppose he handled your mother's business affairs, the estate, and so on."

"Oh, yes. What there was of it."

"Did she own property?"

"Some. North of town. But Howard says it's worthless."

Worthless unless a freeway was coming through. And Tom suspected strongly that was the case. Words boiled up, but he grimly checked them. He couldn't say, Kid, you're getting ripped off. Not if she was going home and marrying the guy. If she really meant to live with this bastard, she'd be better off not knowing.

He got slowly to his feet and stood looking back down the street into the lazy afternoon pandemonium of the marketplace. Abstractedly he tucked truant shirttails into his jeans, tossed his can on a trash pile, and held out his hand. She stood up and slipped her fingers in his. They were cold. He closed his around them warmly.

With slow feet, hand in hand, they climbed the narrow street between rickety, shuttered houses, genteel poor in their lavish fretwork and tropic flowers. At the top was an esplanade and they walked along it, looking out at the azure sea.

The sun was burning down and no one else was around except for a pair of bare-legged children below them, playing happily around an upturned old dory. One lonely sail shone against the glittering horizon, outward bound.

Tom was remembering the motel lobby and the little brown hen in the shapeless coat lugging that impossible suitcase. How he'd laughed at her. Now he could see she'd been frightened. Running.

Well, she'd run a long way. Did she think she could go back to being a little brown hen?

His fingers tightened involuntarily because everything in him rebelled at letting her go. She glanced up. To the misery in her eyes, he said, "Look, I've been wanting to apologize for . . . for that night in the motel, and . . . and yesterday morning. I thought you were someone else."

"Who?"

"It doesn't matter. Just—someone else. Someone very unlike you. I do apologize. Okay?"

"Okay." *But,* she thought, *if he apologizes for holding me and kissing me, I'll die. Not here, not now. It's going to be all I have to remember.*

He didn't apologize. He only walked, and she came with him, down narrow stone streets with jutting weather-faded gables almost meeting overhead. They stood aside to let a group of children pass, two by two, in school uniforms, with skin every shade of brown, shepherded by smiling nuns in dazzling white. Tom bought five chances on a suckling pig while the pig himself grunted through limp lettuce leaves in a crate. Three dark ladies wheeling an old television set in a creaking hand barrow came precariously around a corner. Tom and Jane flattened themselves into a prickly hedge of jungleflame to let them pass while hummingbirds darted overhead, and the starched wings of the ladies' aprons brushed against their arms.

They talked, but not about the dark topic that lay between them, not about Howard, and not about Jane's going home. Quietly Tom said how he'd grown to love Frederiksted and St. Croix, how he'd only come to help his sister when Rob had died unexpectedly, how now he'd like to stay forever. There were things he could do here with his engineer's degree—even simple, mundane things like building sewers and drains, roads and culverts. But they weren't making it, he and Karen. They simply weren't making it. He was going to have to go back to the States, work for his uncle again—just for a while, just to pay off Rob's loan.

"Just for a while," he repeated, and Jane caught the sound of uncertainty in his voice.

She thought of the ten-thousand-dollar check in her bag and wished . . . she wished a lot of things. An old chiché of her

148

mother's came back to her: If wishes were horses, then beggars would ride.

The sun startled them by plopping suddenly below the rim of Frederiksted. Tom looked at his watch and said, "Damn! I had no idea. We've got to get back."

The bus was still sitting before Rustoli's Emporium, except three scrawny chickens were pecking the dirt beneath it and a handsome black giant in white dungarees was hefting crates of lettuce into the back.

"There you go, Tom," he said, slamming the doors. "You all have a mighty nice time now."

Tom nodded, got in, and hoisted Jane up beside him. A wet paper bag sat on the board between them. "Boiled peanuts," he said, and put the warm, moist parcel on the floor at her feet.

They said little on the way back. Jane filled her eyes with the island's beauty, trying frantically to store up the warmth, the lush flowers, the glistening sand, lavender now and blending with the orange and black and gold of the sunset. They stopped beneath tamarind trees by the suddenly familiar shape of Limeberry House. As Tom helped her down, Jane said awkwardly, "Thank you for a—a lovely time."

Tom stopped dead and his hands on hers were tight, his eyes almost angry. "Lovely enough to make you stay?"

Her anguished face kept him from saying more—more of what should not have been said in the first place. He flushed a little, his face set. "Sorry," he muttered, dropping her hands and turning to help unload the lettuce crates.

Her voice shaking a little, she called after him, "See you at the cookout?"

Grimly, not even looking around, he answered, "Maybe. I don't know."

Enveloped in an agony she'd never in her life known before, she went into the foyer and up the stairs.

CHAPTER XIII

As she showered and changed, she found herself praying *Please, God, please, let him be there. Let me see him again.* She didn't even notice that the water was icy cold.

She was running out of clean clothes.

I can launder at home, she thought grimly. *And plod through the snow to work. And have to listen to Sally lying to me about Howard. And let Howard kiss me.*

Oh, God! she thought in anguish. *I wish I'd never come! Why did I have to do this? Why couldn't I leave well enough alone?*

She put on jeans that were fairly clean, a slim-strapped terry top and the same shirt she'd taken off, unbuttoned. It didn't really matter what she wore. She wasn't even hungry, but maybe he would be there. Maybe she'd see him for one last time.

She knew it would be the last time. Karen had already warned them that their flight left very early in the morning.

Nat had strung bright-colored lanterns on the loggia by the pool and Addie was setting tables and lighting candles in small glass jars. A faint tinge of smoke hung over them; with it came a delicious smell of roasting chickens. Karen was hovering over a huge salad bowl, mixing glistening greens with her hands, a towel pinned about her middle. A portable bar had been set up in the arcade with Willard Davis presiding.

He called out cheerfully as Jane entered, "Hey there, little lady, what'll it be?"

"Nothing, thank you."

"Oh, come on!"

"All right. Just a soda."

He poured a can into a glass of ice as elaborately as if serving vintage wine. She smiled her thanks and sat down by his wife. There was a table of snacks set out; beyond it, between the arcade and the pool, other guests were dancing to music from a record player. The air was warm, limpid, and the sky overhead was dazzling with stars.

Mrs. Davis looked up and smiled. She wore a new sundress to show nicely tanned plump shoulders, and was knitting something fleecy.

"A new grandbaby," she said. "Right after we get back, our son says. You look tired, dear. Have a nice day?"

Jane nodded. She had already glanced around; Tom was nowhere to be seen. She sipped her soda, found a potato chip in her hand, ate it, and reached for another. *I may as well get fat again,* she thought.

Karen's busboys were bringing out big trays heaped with hot barbecued chicken and mounds of boiled shrimp. Addie followed with potatoes rich with cheese and cream. She put them down and began her familiar jang-jang-jang on the hanging triangle. Karen stuck a wooden fork and spoon in her salad and stepped out of the way. Russet hair dangled in her eyes; she pushed it back with the clean side of one hand.

"Fill your plates," she urged. "Nat's had those chickens turning and basting since noon." But her mind seemed elsewhere. She gave them an all-encompassing smile, and went back into the house, stripping off her towel as she walked away and absently wiping her hands on it.

Jane got in line with her plate and ate in comparative silence, a babble of voices around her. Afterward she sat by the pool and watched the guests dance, turning, gliding couples varicolored by the soft lanterns. Melissa sneaked over and put on a disco record. She and Michael danced; then Michael fell by the wayside and she went on alone, a jerking, weaving, lithe figure in skintight satin pants. Finally she collapsed breathless to the sound of polite applause. A more conservative record went on again. Michael pulled Melissa to her feet and they wandered out of the lights toward the beach path.

"Youth," murmured Mrs. Davis sympathetically. "It does call girl to boy. At least that's not changed."

"No," said Jane, "it hasn't."

Then suddenly her breath caught. A tall figure strode into the area of soft, shifting light—a figure with broad shoulders and thick dark hair, wearing jeans and a blue shirt now so streaked with grease and dirt that they were hardly recognizable.

"Hang in there, folks," Tom said cheerfully. "Your hot water's back again. Sorry about the inconvenience."

He stripped off dirty cotton gloves to reveal clean hands, picked up a plate, and stacked it high with food. To Jane, he said, grinning, "You forgot to feed me today!" But he walked right by the empty chair at her side and sat down at the pool with some other guests.

The balloon that had suddenly swelled inside her deflated with a dull sputter.

It was over. He'd done his bit, speeded the parting guest with friendly attention, and tried to take the bad taste of Trevor Barry from her mouth. But there were other guests, and as he'd said, his sister and he were in business.

You idiot, she said to herself. *Why do you keep setting yourself up to fall. Why do you imagine things that are not there. Why are you hanging on like a stupid, mooing, lovesick heifer?*

Face facts, Jane Doorn. Get it together. You may as well just go and pack.

She got up, smiled a blurred and encompassing smile, said what she hoped were the proper things to Karen, and went back into the arcade.

The door to Ms. Von Fox's room was half open, the room empty and still. Jane passed it, blinking back tears, went into her own room, and snapped on the light.

There really wasn't much to pack. She laid out her leather coat to carry because it was cold in Quincy, and left the suitcase open on the floor. A few more things in the morning and she would be ready to go.

Then someone else on vacation could have this room, this balcony, the breathtaking view of the beach and the sea and the far-off islands.

She opened the louvered doors, and walked out onto the balcony. The stars were like bits of crystal on black velvet. The white

sand was a rim of silver on which two dark figures walked—
Melissa and Michael. As she looked, they stopped and melted
into one.

Jane choked back the sobs, but the tears streamed anyway,
silent tears cooled by the vanilla breeze that played like light
kisses on her closed eyelids. She clenched her fists on the damp
stone railing, but she could not stop the crying.

Tom Nelson had seen her leave, had felt the hurt as she had
felt it, but grimly resolved to do nothing. It was her life, her
choice. All he might do was muck it up further, and God knew,
she didn't need that.

He started down the path to his windmill. As soon as he was
out of sight of the guests, he pulled off his greasy shirt and let
the cool breeze touch his body. *Get cleaned up,* he was telling
himself. *Have a drink. There are other women in the world.*

Then he saw her, starkly alone above him—and he knew that
right now there wasn't any other woman for him.

He cursed silently as she cried. He cursed himself, Trevor
Barry, the Howard turkey that was at the bottom of all her
misery. A better man would have left her up there, and gone on
about his business. But he was no hero.

He put one foot on the elbow of the drainpipe, another on the
lip of the arcade, and heaved himself to within reach of the
railing. "If you don't give me a hand," he grunted, "I'm going
to fall and break a leg—and that will be a damned sight less than
romantic."

Her eyes had flown open at the sound of breaking vines.
Incredulously she stared, tears still wet on her cheeks. Then at
the sound of his voice she reached out in terror, clutching at his
lean brown body, feeling the muscles slide beneath her fingers as
he heaved himself upward, threw a leg over the rail, and stood
erect. Panting, he towered over her, saying, "Damn. I'm getting
too old for this sort of thing. Why the hell did you run off? I
wanted to dance with you."

"I—I don't dance very well," she said shakily. "Hardly at all."

"With this modern stuff, who can tell?"

But it was all words, just words. He flicked at her wet cheeks with his finger. His voice was rough. "What's all this nonsense?"

Anger spurted through her. How could he ask? How dare he ask?

She stepped away from him—the latent power in that deep bare chest, the odor of grease and sweat and sun and man. "Don't take that tack with me!" she said bitterly. "I'm not Melissa—"

He knew what he could do. He could cut across rudely. *I'll say you're not! Melissa's flat chested and has no fanny, and you're about the most gorgeous armful of woman I've seen in years!* He could scoop her up and kiss her and stroke her and let her struggle until, outraged, she hit him again, like the first time, and ran off completely cured of Tom Nelson.

But he couldn't do it. He wasn't that keen on self-sacrifice; besides, both he and Trev Barry doing a number on her wasn't fair to some guy who might come along later—even that Howard turkey.

Instead he said, "Of course you're not Melissa. She's not in my ball park either."

"What do you mean—your ball park?"

"I mean I don't usually make a habit of romancing engaged girls—unless they demonstrate that they are very *un*engaged. What I'm trying to do, you idiot, is be halfway decent to you."

The air suddenly went out of her in a rush.

Quietly now she said, "I guess I don't want you to be—be decent to me. I guess that's the problem."

Also quietly he answered, "It's your decision."

The breeze fluttered her shirt, blew his dark hair softly across his face. He was a still brown giant, waiting.

She made a sound he couldn't define. Then she stuck out a hand. It was brown too, much browner than when he'd first seen it. "Good-bye, Tom," she said hopelessly.

He took the hand and shook it. She turned and went back inside her room. He threw a long, grease-stained leg over the railing.

Then he smashed the rail with his fist. "Goddamnit all to

155

hell!" he cried, putting the leg down and taking one long angry stride toward her door.

One was enough. She was already coming back, running into the arms she saw were open wide. He caught her up in them, holding her with more hunger than he'd ever felt in his life for any woman.

She gave herself up to him fully, totally; he felt the response of her mouth on his, the willing satin of the warm breasts inside the terry top against his stroking, hungry hands, the rounded press of her body to his lean and aching flanks. The world spun like a crazy thing.

He gritted his teeth. He made himself relax, let go, put her down, walk away. From the damp stones of the railing he turned and said hoarsely, "Stand right there, and let me tell you something. Kissing you is not enough. Holding you is not enough. The way I feel, it is never going to be enough. The most magnificent thing in my life right now would be to have you in bed with me, that whole beautiful length of you all mine. But I don't go to bed without a commitment. And you can't give me one. Can you, Jane?"

She stood where he'd left her. He saw the translucent look of a woman being loved fade from her face, leaving it pale in the moonlight. Her voice shook.

"No," she said.

"Good-bye, Jane," he answered, and this time when he threw a leg over the railing he meant it. She heard vines tear, the sound of a body landing lightly, and he was gone. She could not see the hand with its bleeding knuckles where he savagely smashed each tree trunk all the way to his mill.

With numb feet she walked back inside. Her aching head echoed with Edna St. Vincent Millay's poem about her candle burning at both ends, how it would not last the night, but what a lovely light it made.

Her candle was burnt out. It was time to go home. To Howard. And the box.

CHAPTER XIV

They were at the luggage carrousel in St. Louis before Jane began to notice the cold. She sensed it, more than felt it, from the wind-reddened faces and the heavy coats on the people around her. Then Melissa, standing with Michael next to Jane, suddenly cried "Dickie!" and launched herself into the arms of a tall young man in a western-type brush jacket. Jane noticed then that he had a powder of unmelted snow on his shoulders. "My mother's down here shopping," Dickie said, "I told your dad I'd pick you up." But his eyes were on Michael with all the cordiality of a hostile tomcat.

Unperturbed, Melissa said, "Dick, Michael. Michael, Dick." Then she squealed "Greg!" and turned from Dickie to the bear hug of a willowy specimen with two tennis racquet cases. "Greg, how marvelous to see you! Fellows, amuse each other. I just have to talk to Greg; it's been so *long!*"

Dick and Michael looked at each other. Dick said gruffly, "I've got a fake I. D.; I'll buy you a beer."

Michael hoisted his duffel bag onto his shoulder. "That sounds like a winner," he said, and they went off together.

This time Jane recognized her own luggage. She plucked it from the moving belt and went down the concourse to Air Illinois. She was far too numb with her own problems to give Melissa even a backward glance. The Melissas of this world fell on their feet. It was the Janes who broke.

The snow crackled beneath her shoes as Jane boarded the Air Illinois plane. The air was so cold it hurt her lungs, and it was filled with lazy flakes. They fell in clumps of cotton and immediately the ground disappeared. Behind her Jane heard Mrs. Davis give a small gasp and Willard murmur "Now, now, Madge." Jane wondered in a fragmented sort of way if crashing in a snowstorm might not be a solution.

However the brief trip was without incident. The snow at

Baldwin Field, Quincy, was deeper, wind-rowed into heaps that were blindingly white in the gray light of midday. Long icicles hung from the terminal building, and as they rode into town, people on the streets had a harried, pinched look, their necks swathed in high collars.

The courtesy limo dropped Jane off at the garage. She paid her bill in cash, was rewarded by glowing promises of eternal health for part of the car, and drove it out into the street, across the gunmetal waters of the Mississippi toward home.

One part of her mind was numb. That was Tom's part; and she was already trying to seal it off, thicken the scar tissue.

Perhaps years later she would be brave enough to break the seal, to take out the memory and look at it. Perhaps by then it would only give off a faint perfume, like old roses. But not now. Now it bled.

At three o'clock, as an attendant filled her gas tank, she took out Howard's ring and put it back on.

At seven thirty she turned off the Interstate and drove down the brightly lighted, tinsel-hung street of her own hometown.

In the week she'd been gone, Christmas had bloomed with a vengeance. Plastic candles swung from each lamppost. Colored lights swayed across the intersections. Vacuous Santa masks dangled from store windows. Two thousand light bulbs outlined the wings of the municipal windmill—all of them blinking. Over the entire town hung an inescapable, tinkling, chiming, mellifluous miasma of *Joyeux Noël*. Even her own street seemed to have developed a nervous tic of elf lights.

The Doorn driveway was a blanket of snow crisscrossed by the paper carrier on his daily rounds and various marauding dogs. Jane kicked off her shoes, tugged on the old boots, and, leaving her car running in the street, slogged up the driveway to tug open the garage doors. With some urging and a familiar rasp, they opened, loosing a cold damp rush of air at her face. A sliver of light showed briefly between her neighbor's kitchen curtains. Well, the news is out, she thought acidly, following her own trail back to the street. Jane Doorn is home.

By judicious nursing she coaxed her car up into the garage,

and banged the door down again. The kitchen lock stuck, of course; it always had. But finally she was able to carry her luggage into the house. She found it colder and drearier than the garage. She drew open drapes and the effect remained the same: damp, cold, and empty. Still on her bed was the heap of clothes dumped from her old suitcase. Was that only seven days ago?

Tears pricked her eyelids. She blinked them back, put down her new luggage, and went back into the living room to slide up the thermostat. There was an audible hesitation, then a reluctant var-room as the furnace started up.

Thank God for small favors, she said silently, then sighed, picked up the cold phone, and began to dial.

It was what she'd been preparing herself to do all day. Yet when the rings began to sound, she was suddenly dry mouthed and in a panic.

"Howard Van Tassel speaking."

She swallowed.

He repeated, "Van Tassel's."

It finally came out. "Howard? I'm home." Then she added belatedly, "This is Jane."

"Oh. How are you?"

"I'm fine. How are you?"

"Well, thank you. Of course we've both had colds." (The "we've" was self-explanatory, if you knew Howard.) "Did you get your car?"

"Yes, just today. It runs fine though."

"It ought to run fine!"

There was a curious silence. Pathetically she was thinking, *Please, say you've missed me!*

He didn't. Instead he said, "I assume you're home to stay." Not "hope"—which would have made all the difference. Why did it have to be "assume"?

"Yes, I am." The bottomless-pit sound was in her voice, but he didn't notice. He had his own problems.

"I'm very tired," he said. "Is it all right if I don't come over this evening?"

A reprieve! "Oh, of course. I'm tired too. I was thinking of going straight to bed."

"Fine. The Jaycee Christmas breakfast is in the morning at nine. Suppose I pick you up for that? I assume you aren't going back to work until Monday?"

"No. No, I'm not. The breakfast will be fine."

"Is the house all right? If I'd known when you were coming, I could have turned the heat up."

There was reproof in that. She ignored it. "That's all right. It seems to be heating nicely. I'll see you in the morning."

"A little before nine. Good night, Jane."

"Good night."

She hung up slowly, relieved because he wasn't coming tonight, hurt because he hadn't wanted to come.

So Howard's arms and Howard's kisses were put off until tomorrow. Yet she had to get used to them again. She had to get used to everything again.

Somehow the phone conversation had been totally different from what she'd expected. She thought he'd be angry. After all, he had made that useless trip to Quincy, although he didn't know she knew it.

Perhaps he thought she'd be the one to be angry—about Sally. Perhaps he was just giving himself time to come up with a good story.

Anyway, she said to herself, and was suddenly desperately truthfully bone weary. *Anyway, he knows I'm home.*

If I can only get to sleep . . .

She hadn't slept last night. Not at all. And she couldn't bear another night like that one. Not until she could look at the whole thing more clearly, without hurting, without wanting the impossible, without breaking down and sobbing like a bereft child.

She walked into the bedroom, took off her leather coat, and hung it like an elegant stranger among the serviceable clothes in her closet. She creamed her face, looking into a mirror that reflected a stranger until plain Jane Doorn looked back at herself with all the makeup smeared on tissue. Except—she was different. There was no escaping it. Her hair was darker. She was

160

tanned. The lifeless look was gone. She was tired, she was aching —but there was life in those smudged eyes. Would Howard notice?

So many times in past years, when she'd been filled with nameless hurt, she'd put on her pink flannel nightie and burrowed into her small soft bed, shutting out all sights and sounds except the comforting fantasies she made up inside her head.

Tonight it wouldn't work. The nightgown was uncomfortable, the bed too soft, and the fantasies wouldn't come.

She'd gone away a child and come back at least half a woman —the yearning, searching half.

At three in the morning she finally dropped off into a restless sleep, but she woke up again at seven. She lay quite still, stunned with disappointment. Limeberry was far away, Limeberry with its white sands and warm sun. Tom was far away. All she had now was soft snow hitting her windows, and the prospect of starting her life all over again with Howard.

She made up her face very carefully and brushed her hair until it fell into place like a silk curtain, but she didn't have quite enough courage to wear the red dress Howard had failed to recognize her in. Besides, it was snowing again. The toast slacks and sweater would do very well. And the leather coat. She would not give up the leather coat, she told herself, vaguely aware that certain of her new clothes might be required to disappear—to keep the peace.

It was a quarter of nine when Howard came slogging to the door, bundled in his heavy storm coat like a portly teddy bear. She opened it while he was stamping his feet on the porch. Her heart beating, she said, "Hello, Howard."

"Damned snow," he grunted, peeling off flopping overshoes. "If it keeps up, I suppose I'll have to have Charlie shovel the bank roof again—"

Then he looked up. His eyes widened. Then they narrowed. "Good God," he said. "What have you done?"

"Just changed my hair," Jane answered uneasily. She tried to make her voice light. "Come in before you freeze."

He walked inside, still dangling his overshoes. "Wait," she said, "I'll get a paper."

She spread the paper out on the floor. Howard dropped the overshoes with a plop. He was still staring, but now his eyes had focus, and they made Jane even more uneasy. "It just takes getting used to," she said.

"It's more than the hair. Your face is different."

"Nonsense. It's the same face."

"It's not. It's—painted."

Shades of 1920! Surprising herself, Jane said, "It's made up, Howard. There's a difference there too."

"Mother won't like it."

"Do you like it?" That was forthright; a small glow of anger was making her courageous.

He hesitated, frowning. "You look like—like—" He was close to saying Sally and she knew it—she was sure of it. Instead he said rather limply, "A stranger." Then he added the genuine bottom line to it all. "People are going to talk."

"Haven't they, already?" she asked a little stubbornly.

"Yes, they have. You've made it difficult for me, Jane."

"I'm sorry. I didn't mean to do that. I just had to—to get off by myself."

She reached out and touched his arm appealingly. He was still looking at her, and now there was a speculative look he couldn't disguise.

"That's what I told them. Did you?"

"Did I what?"

"Go off by yourself?"

She knew then, unmistakably, that like a tomcat, he could sense a difference that went deeper than cosmetics and hair styles. Inside, besides being hurt and angry, Howard was bristling suspiciously.

"Yes," she said, "I did." She didn't elaborate.

He patently swallowed his suspicions. Right before her eyes. Once again she felt this new ambivalence in him toward her and couldn't explain it—unless Sally was the cause, and that remained to be seen. "Anyway," he said, "you're back."

He put his arms around her, and drew her against the thick fleece of his coat. She smelt the familiar odor of deodorant soap and aftershave and lifted her face obediently. Then she felt a moment of pure terror, for his embrace was not familiar; it was more exploratory, more explicit—and she wasn't ready for that. Not with Howard! If she was to regain her former passive tolerance, she had to be led to it gradually, and right now Howard was pushing.

She tried to step back, tried turning it into a joke, saying, "My goodness, not before breakfast!"

But she sensed immediately that resistance had been a mistake. It only solidified his suspicions; submission would have been better.

He let her go. "All right," he said. "Get your coat." He turned away so that she couldn't see his face. "The house okay?"

"Yes, it seems to be."

She came out of the bedroom, pulling on her leather coat, and his eyes widened in further shock.

But Howard did not say How much did that cost? a question so standard that Jane had already framed an answer. He only murmured, "That's very nice," as he opened the door. Perhaps the sight of her old snow boots reassured him.

The bank car was running at the curb, throwing out a gray stream of exhaust into the cold air. Mrs. Van Tassel wasn't sitting in the front seat—although she had been. Jane could smell her perfume.

"I dropped Mother off early," Howard said. "She says the later arrivals get yesterday's sweet rolls." He put the car in drive and moved it cautiously toward the intersection. "She may not recognize you."

But she did recognize Jane. Jane saw her lips narrow as she swiftly took in the full picture—hair, makeup, coat. But she accepted the daughterly peck on her cheek and said nothing. *Well, well,* said Jane to herself. *What is going on here?*

Could Howard possibly have missed her so much, been so concerned about her welfare, that he was willing to take her back on any terms? And could he have told his mother so?

That's too much of a pipe dream, Jane told herself, but wished heartily that it were true.

At the breakfast, assorted Jaycee gentlemen slapped pancakes and scrambled eggs into Howard's plate, then looked up and saw Jane. To a man they blinked, said things like, "Why, Jane. Welcome back!" Then they nudged each other, clear down the serving line.

Jane enjoyed it. Howard grinned about it sheepishly. Mother Van Tassel didn't like it at all.

She was going shopping downtown with her friend Grace. Howard turned from pecking at her cheek to see one of the Jaycees helping Jane into her expensive leather coat. He'd never before noticed the sensual line of breast and waist a woman exposes thrusting her arms into a garment. He knew how Jane was built; he didn't appreciate the whole town knowing.

I can't allow this, Howard told himself seriously.

He bumped into old Mr. Josten just for the reassurance of hearing him toady and say, "Oh, excuse me!" Then he took Jane's arm and led her firmly across the dirty snow to the car again.

"Would you like to stop by the bank with me?" he asked genially. "You can redeposit your cash, and I can take care of that McIlhenny check."

"I don't have either with me," Jane answered calmly. "I'm not overdrawn, am I?"

"Oh, no. No, but—"

"Then I'll do it later. Or, if you like, I can walk home from the bank."

"No, that's not necessary."

He drove her home through the soft falling snow. Home seemed safest until he could digest the new situation, decide what had to be done. One thing he knew for certain: he couldn't afford to lose control. The old Jane had been so passive, so easy to dominate. This new Jane—frankly, she alarmed him.

Where the hell had she been? Why had she gone there? And what were going to be the repercussions? Damn. He hated the unknown. . . .

He had to reestablish his dominance. It was as simple as that. And as difficult.

Had she been with a man? His Jane! She'd been his for so long, like a piece of furniture. It shook him to discover he could be jealous—and that was dangerous too.

She was sitting there silently, her hands folded in her lap. But her mind was far away from the town, from him. He could tell. He didn't like it.

He pulled to the curb, said casually, "Mother wants us to dinner this evening. We need to make some plans."

She turned and looked at him. Suddenly he felt nervous. He smoothed his silky moustache with one hand, tapping the wheel with the other. "The church sanctuary is going to be renovated. Mother would like to see us marry at the old altar—where she and Dad were married."

There was really nothing wrong with that—in fact, the sentiment was understandable. Yet Jane felt her heart squeeze. "When?" she asked.

"Right after the first of the year."

"Howard, I couldn't possibly be ready—"

But he was reaching over and patting her cold hand.

"Now, now," he said kindly, "we've been talking about it. I think we can work something out."

"Christmas is only three days away!"

"Don't worry. We'll talk tonight. See if you can get a little rest, Jane. You look tired."

Tired was not precisely the word. Jane got out into the snow, gave him a faint smile, and slogged toward the porch. Her neighbor was erecting a plastic Santa Claus and plywood reindeer on his roof; he called down, "Hi! Have a good time?"

"Yes, thank you."

"Mighty pretty suntan. Where'd you go—Florida?"

"You're close."

"You picked a poor time to come back. This snow is never going to stop. Hey, Jane!"

She paused. He came to the edge of his roof and peered down at her. "Will you sell your house?"

It took a moment to realize he was serious. Puzzled, she tried to sound light. "Why, Mr. Surrey? Do you want to buy it?"

"Not me. My oldest kid. He's getting transferred back here. And since I'd noticed Howard showing it to a couple of other people, I thought, hell, no harm in asking. I didn't figure how you and he would live here anyway."

Shock had turned Jane rigid. How dare Howard do such a thing—without so much as consulting her!

Evenly she answered, "I'll keep you in mind," and went on into the house. All of a sudden she had a savage headache.

She took three aspirin, and lay down on the couch, her hands pressed to her temples. The silence pressed too—an echoing silence that had a smell of dampness, loneliness, and misery.

Despite herself, Jane felt her anger slip away. She could see Howard's reasoning. They were getting married soon. Howard had hinted about one of the new tri-levels over by the country club; and in any event, they wouldn't need this place.

Marrying. After New Year—less than two weeks away!

Yet the sooner they got on with it, the better it would be for her. She would be forced cruelly to forget Limeberry, to blot it out. And that was what she needed.

Wearily she hauled herself to her feet and went to do laundry. In the bottom of her suitcase she found the crumpled, brown remains of that sprig of oleander.

She went into the bathroom and made herself flush it down the toilet.

CHAPTER XV

Laundering the things from Limeberry was a bad experience, and quite a few tears were shed in the basement at Jane's house. She hung the lovely white dress in her mother's closet, folded away the shorts and halter tops, and put the satin robe and nightgown in a drawer. Common sense told her she had the beginnings of a trousseau if she'd only use her head.

Practical. That's what she had to be. Yet the idea of Howard's chubby hands on that satin nightdress didn't make her blush. She shivered.

She simply had to get over that nonsense!

She dressed carefully for the evening at the Van Tassel's. There would be a fine line between wearing what she liked and humoring Mother.—And since Mother, in all probability, would live to be a hearty hundred and one, Jane had better start setting ground rules now.

How much simpler it would be if she could count on Howard's support. But she knew she couldn't.

We are both infants, she thought soberly, *each in our own way. Howard thinks he's grown up. I know I haven't.*

He came in through the garage about six, stamping snow from his overshoes and waiting for her in the kitchen. She'd put on her old brown coat, which was not only warmer but pleased him to see it. He kissed her warmly, and this time she braced herself to submit, but he stopped there. Mother expected people on time.

The Van Tassels never ate in the kitchen, always in the dining room, with Great-grandmother Someone's china and the flat sterling that had to be wiped dry with a soft cloth and slipped into individual felt sheaths each time it was used. Jane knew the routine well. If, once more, she felt it was a little much for indifferent meatloaf and canned peas, once more she didn't say so. Howard served from warmed plates stacked at his place. His mother, elegant in a pearl choker and large earrings, dispensed weak tea. Jane ate and drank politely and waited for the bomb to drop.

It's my life, she kept telling herself sturdily, *and I must make it clear: I will not sit up, bark, or roll over.*

Even so, the meal's aftermath began badly. She got a lipstick smudge on a napkin. She knew Mrs. Van Tassel's keen gray eyes saw it, although she said nothing. Punishment came later when she found herself allotted the awful burned-on meatloaf pan to wash while her hostess daintily polished silver.

Howard, of course, was reclining in the living room, with a cigar and the television. He actually beamed when they entered, saying, "Well, this is nice. My two favorite girls!"—a strikingly unoriginal remark that pleased neither of them. He fussed over his mother, adjusting her hassock, turning the television brightness to suit her, and putting a pillow to her back. Jane, as usual, took the small armchair, and looked around at the Van Tassel decor with more than her usual disfavor. Inevitably Barry Greathouse came to mind with its airy space and graceful furniture. Here, everything was dark, heavy, and lathered with knobby carving.

Even an apartment, Jane was thinking to herself, *a very small apartment will be better than this place. I shouldn't mind a small apartment. I can make it if it's just Howard and me.*

"—and Pastor says we may have the Chapel the twenty-ninth," Mrs. Van Tassel was saying to her son.

"Very nice," said Howard. "That's a Sunday, isn't it? We can manage, can't we, Jane?"

Jane looked at him blankly.

As though to a small child, he said, "We can get married on the twenty-ninth, can't we?"

It was impossible to conceal her dismay. "Howard!" she said, "that's even sooner than we agreed on. I've done nothing! There are no invitations, no caterer, no wedding dress—"

"If you had been home, my dear," said Mrs. Van Tassel suavely, "you could have done those things already. But you weren't, you see. So the burden fell on Howie and me. However," she added with a sort of royal kindness, "I'm sure you will approve of what we've decided. I find it such a blessing to have Howard marrying a sensible girl."

Howard came over and sat down on the arm of Jane's chair. He patted her suddenly pale cheek. "Just the details," he said, and from the tone of his voice she realized she was being soothed. "A small wedding party—because of your poor mother's death, of course—so handwritten invitations will do quite well. William's cater morning ceremonies nicely. Morning, because our airline reservations are for the afternoon. So you see, dearest, all you have to be is the beautiful bride. And you will be," he added suddenly in her ear, "—beautiful," and kissed her.

From the other side of the room his mother said coldly, "And I do hope that awful brown has faded. I should hate your going down the aisle looking like a—a tennis player."

Suddenly Jane realized two things: Howard had never before kissed her in front of his mother, and his mother did not like it. She was, in fact, jealous.

Just what I need right now, Jane thought dismally. "You've been very kind—seeing to all these things for me." *Good grief, what a hypocrite you are becoming, Jane!* "But—what in the world shall I wear?"

The moment the words were out, she knew she'd trapped herself further. Howard took a deep breath, and answered with awe, "Jane, you are marrying the son of one of the most wonderful Moms in the world! My mother says you may wear her wedding dress."

Jane remembered Mrs. Van Tassel's wedding dress—that ghastly slipper-satin 1940's number with the football shoulderpads and the mobcap veil.

"It has such happy memories," said Mrs. Van Tassel complacently.

What choice did Jane have? She was surrounded, boxed in. If she said no—in fact, no to anything, they'd never forgive her—neither of them. It was too high a price to pay for trivialities. There would be bigger things to struggle for later. She'd better save her strength.

She tried on the awful dress, standing on a chair while Mrs.

169

Van Tassel stuck pins in her, enduring the smell of musty age and moldy stiffening. Then, back in her own clothes with the gown cradled in Mrs. Van Tassel's arms, Howard was allowed into the room again.

His mother had shooed him out, being coy about the groom not seeing the bride in her wedding gown. Jane, however, knew damned well he'd lurked around the corner peeking, probably lusting for the sight of something bare.

Sadly she realized, *If I loved him, I'd have shown him something. I'd have wanted him to see me. Oh, God, how can I turn this farce into something good?*

"Howard," said his mother, and there was no denying the small, satisfied smile around the corners of her mouth, "why don't you take Jane upstairs and show her the rooms?"

"Good idea," said Howard jovially, and held out his hand. "Come along, Jane."

Jane followed obediently; nonetheless, she asked, "What rooms?"

"Ours."

Stunned, Jane stopped dead. "What?"

"Ours," he repeated and tugged at her. "Where we'll live. A bedroom and a bath and a little place she says we can have for a den. Of course we'll eat with Mother."

"No," said Jane. "Howard, no! Oh, Howard, please—"

"Shh!" he said, almost angrily. "She'll hear! Wait until she's gone into the kitchen. There. Now, Jane, we have to be reasonable."

Her knees would not even bend. She looked up at him, pale-faced, almost ghostly in the dim stairwell. "Howard, I'm sorry," she whispered, "but I just can't. You don't understand—"

"Jane." He interrupted her, and his voice had changed, sounding almost vulnerable. "Please, Jane, come on up a moment. I have to tell you something."

Reluctantly she followed him into the upper hallway. He didn't turn on any lights and it was pitch dark except for the light from below throwing long skinny spindle shadows on the opposite wall.

He had one hand; now he took the other. "It's temporary," he whispered. "As God is my witness, I swear. Just not right now. Not until spring. Can't you manage until spring, Jane?"

She swallowed. "Howard, what's wrong?"

He hesitated. His face in the half shadows was wan, pathetic. Finally he said, "I've—lost quite a lot of money. It's temporary too. I swear, Jane. I've already made it back, but I won't take payment until spring. Then we can afford one of those tri-levels. But now I'm barely hanging by my teeth. It's the God's truth, Jane."

"Your mother doesn't know?"

"No, she doesn't. Just you. Help me, Jane."

It was a strange thing, Jane thought. Against force she would have stood adamant. But Howard was playing upon her sympathy. And, more important, for the first time he'd told her something his mother did not know. She was in his confidence, and his mother was not.

On such small things as that perhaps they could build a marriage, she thought, and found herself putting her arms around his chubby shoulders. Trust. Honesty. If she could only have those . . .

"Howard," she whispered, "thank you."

Not understanding, but appreciative of the suddenly willing proximity of her enticing body, he kissed her. Jane submitted, as she'd promised herself she would. Howard didn't notice her reluctance.

He took her home about ten, but didn't linger. He needed to get to the pharmacy before it closed; Mother felt one of her migraines coming on. Jane went into the kitchen, kicked off her boots, and put the kettle on for coffee. A cup of instant in her hands, she padded to the old living room TV, turned on the news, and sat down, nursing the coffee but not drinking it, watching the screen but not seeing it.

She'd committed herself to a wedding in which she was given no choice, a dress she hated, and living with a mother-in-law who was jealous of her. Not a very positive future.

Yet Howard—prancing, stuffy, egotistical Howard—had

171

shown a crack in the self-assured face he turned to the world. He'd asked for help. He had confided in her. He'd trusted her—not because he had to, but because he wanted to.

It was a poor substitute for love, perhaps, but it was a beginning.

The telephone rang at Jane's elbow. Automatically she picked it up. "Hello."

The tinny sound of long distance shimmered in her ear. "Jane?"

"Yes." Then the cup splashed; she put it down because she was shaking. "Tom?"

"That's right." His faraway voice sounded harsh, clipped. "How are you?"

"I'm—I'm fine."

"Damn it all to hell, I don't want social niceties! How are you?"

"I—I'm okay. Truly. Where are you?"

"I'm in Quincy again, trying to bail out a sinking hostel. Where the hell else would I be? Karen wanted me to call."

That was like a slap in the face, which was the way he meant it. She stiffened. "Thank her for me," she said. "Tell her I'm being married on the twenty-ninth."

"Congratulations!" he said savagely and hung up.

I will not cry, she said to herself, *I will not cry.*

But she did.

Far away in his motel room, Tom Nelson stared at the mute phone with storm-blackened eyes, his mouth a tight line. Then the line broke, and he put his head in his hands. He shouldn't have called. It had been a calculated gamble and he'd lost. She was going to marry that lout. So she'd just have to take her lumps—and he, his.

He still thought it wasn't his right to tell her about her boyfriend's chicanery. Maybe she already knew. Maybe she had enough feelings for the bastard to make it unimportant. Women could be so damned forgiving. Or maybe she had enough feelings for him that *knowing* would only tear her up, ruin whatever

172

peace of mind she might have had if Tom Nelson had kept his fat mouth shut.

Tom only knew what *his* feelings were for her, and how incredible they would seem to Jane in the light of what he'd done to her, time and time again. What a bastard *he* must have seemed!

He'd lost. That was it. There'd be other girls who'd melt against him, who'd willingly blend their soft bodies to his. But it wouldn't be any good. Because it wouldn't be Jane.

He couldn't even go out and get drunk. He couldn't afford it. So he went to bed, and woke up hugging his pillow.

CHAPTER XVI

In her naiveté, Jane thought Limeberry would fade like a dream. It didn't. She still awoke each morning listening for the whish-whish of Addie's broom, the soft sound of the sea on sand. And each morning she had to readjust her heart to the truth: There was no sand, no sea—only snow and cold, and Howard.

Their approaching marriage was announced in church. The Van Tassels being people of consequence, pre-nuptial parties were hastily organized, and Jane began to accumulate gifts of considerable value. Mrs. Van Tassel displayed them in her living room on a long table covered with the tablecloth Jane had brought back from St. Croix. Each gift seemed only another millstone around Jane's neck.

Mr. Elbert apologetically asked her to work three days—only to finish the annual stockholders report. Of course he had already agreed to give her a second week off for the trip to Las Vegas.

Sally greeted Jane the first day by saying, "I really didn't think you'd be back."

"I gathered," answered Jane, and left it at that. But they both knew, and the old camaraderie was gone—if it had ever existed. Perhaps it hadn't. *I've been such a simple soul,* Jane thought. *Perhaps she's been having me on for years and I just didn't realize.*

Sally had a new ring—a square-cut emerald, really quite beautiful—and she was mysterious about its source, but made certain it overshadowed Howard's small diamond on Jane's finger.

There were times, in fact, when Jane knew that if she didn't have the consolation of believing Howard was beginning to love her, she honestly couldn't have gone on. Only the thought of helping him sustained her. She gave him the McIlhenny check, wishing it didn't have to go toward paying off her mother's medical bills. At least Howard didn't have to pay them. Jane intended to redeposit the remains of her two thousand, but she put that off, hating to have him know how profligate she'd been when he was in need. She began, too, running out of some of her new cosmetics, and not replacing them. They seemed so extravagant. She also wished Howard would postpone the Las Vegas trip, but he said they needed to keep up appearances. Jane supposed that was right.

In the early mornings, with the cold of the heavy snow burdening the silent trees, and the longing for Limeberry on her, she acknowledged what she was trying to do—bury herself in Howard's life. She must do it to survive.

The wedding was set for Sunday at eleven thirty, after regular services. On Friday afternoon, after the bank closed, the bank employees gave their boss and his fiancée a small party and presented them with a silver tea service. When everyone was gone, Howard helped Jane rewrap the gift and carry it out to her car.

She slid onto the cold seat, and started the car. Howard bent and kissed her briefly. "I have an hour or so's more work," he said. "Tying up loose ends. Mother wants to check some details. Shall I call you about eight and we'll all get together?"

Jane really didn't need another dose of Mother—not on her last free night. "I need to pack," she said. "The rehearsal is tomorrow evening; I can't do it then."

He nodded, shrugged. He was really being sweet about things. He bent and kissed her again. "Much nicer without that lipstick," he murmured, and let his hand slide suggestively over her breast. "Two more nights," he said. "Can you last?"

She managed to smile. "I have great endurance," she replied, and put the car in drive. Her last sight of Howard was of him standing on the curb before the deserted bank blowing his nose.

Sadly she thought, *It's not can I last until the wedding, but can I last afterward. I can't close my eyes and pretend he's Tom. I can't start off marriage that way. And even if I did pretend, it wouldn't work. He's too plump, too short, too lax. I've been in Tom's arms. I know the feeling of strength and suppleness, of Tom's shoulders, of his back muscles sliding beneath my hands.*

176

"Oh, damn!" she cried out, and beat the steering wheel with one gloved fist. *Stop it, stop it, you idiot! You mustn't do this to yourself; it's insane. You wanted something to remember—well, you got more than you bargained for!*

She pulled up into her driveway and sat for a moment, fighting back tears. Then with a shiver and a deep, tearing sigh, she opened the door, slid her feet out on the shoveled path, and reached for her purse.

It wasn't there.

Good grief, I left it in Howard's office. I'm locked out of my house!

She didn't want to drive back downtown again. She didn't want to see Howard again—not right now. But she really had no choice. All the doors and windows were firmly locked, and no one else had a key.

"Damn," she said again, reclosing the car door and backing out of the driveway.

The main lobby of the bank was silent and deserted. Now what could she do? There were a few passersby on the street, but she hated making a spectacle of herself. She went around to the back lobby off the parking lot.

She pressed her face against the heavy glass, and looked in both directions. She could barely glimpse a bar of light beneath Howard's office door. Almost automatically she pressed against the brass handle—and, to her astonishment, it moved! It wasn't locked!

The warmth of the rear corridor poured out as she entered, wiping her feet carefully before she stepped on Howard's new imitation oriental runner. Two silk prints of plum blossoms flanked his office door, guarded by a pair of snarling and extraordinarily ugly China temple dogs. She tapped lightly, and got no answer. Of course he could be in the executive board room just beyond his office.

She pushed at the door. It wasn't locked, but Howard wasn't at his desk. Silently she went across the thick plush rug, and opened the board room door.

177

Howard's back was to Jane, being encircled by Sally's arms inside his shirt. He was very occupied by the contents of Sally's unbuttoned blouse. Sally was not as well endowed as Jane, but he didn't seem to be finding this a problem at all.

"Good grief!" Jane said simply.

Sally's head was thrown back with enjoyment at Howard's nuzzling, but at the sound of Jane's voice her eyes popped wide open.

Then, inexplicably, she smiled. "Howie, darling," she murmured, "we have company."

But Howard had heard too. He half turned, his chubby hands still clutching their amorous treasures, and his face was a perfect mask of horror. In one of those ridiculous moments of truth, Jane thought, *He certainly hasn't minded Sally's lipstick.* It was streaked across his mouth and chin.

"Oh, my God!" he said. For one brief minute he seemed frozen, transfixed, immobile. Then he seemed almost to lunge away from Sally, coming toward Jane, saying, "Jane, Jane, it's not what it seems! She forced her way in here. She enticed me—"

"Oh, can it, Howie," Sally interrupted rudely. "We're fairly caught." She began rebuttoning her blouse.

He spun back and hit her savagely across the face with his open hand. She reeled into a chair; he stood over her, panting, saying hysterically, "She's lying. She'll tell nothing but lies, don't listen to her, Jane. Jane, she's nothing but a three-dollar broad!"

Sally put her fingers to her mouth. They came away bloody. In a soft voice she said, "That did it. That did it." She came up out of the chair like an avenging angel, slipped by him and stood at Jane's side. "Look at him!" she spat. "Look at him! There's two years of my life standing there like a wet macaroni! And damned little I've got out of it too, except a few lousy bucks here and there and this—to hush me up!" She thrust out her hand with the emerald at him. He snatched at the hand, but she grabbed it back. "Well, it won't hush me now, buster! A three-dollar broad, am I? We'll see!"

I'm imagining this, Jane thought dully. *It's not happening.* In a flat voice, she said, "It doesn't matter. I'm leaving."

Howard came toward her and she added, "Don't touch me!"

"Jane!" he said, almost in tears.

Sally laughed. "I'll go too," she said. "I want to tell you about the McIlhenny people, dumb Jane, and how Howard here has been ripping you off. There's a freeway going across your land, you idiot, and a shopping center next to it. That piece out there is worth a mint, and guess who's been sucking it all in! You'd better grab on to something, Howie, darling, because I'm not through yet!"

Howard's fingers closed on his onyx paperweight. He screamed, "Get out! Get out!" and threw it with all his strength. It just missed Sally's head. She went pale.

"All right," she said, and laughed viciously. "I'll go. Miss Priss, here, knows where to find me if she needs to hear more."

She grabbed up her coat. Jane stepped aside numbly to let her pass. The door hissed shut with a stately precision and they both stared at it.

"Jane—" Howard said humbly.

"No, Howard," Jane answered. "Enough has been said already."

She went back into his office, and picked up her purse from a chair. How calm I am, she thought. *How quiet. I feel just as I did when Mother died.*

Suddenly her hands were seized. Howard was on his knees before her, clinging, holding her hands against his wet face, kissing them, crying, "Jane, don't leave me! You can't leave me. I admit I lied. It was Mother's idea. Jane, you don't know how my mother can be. Jane, there's plenty of money, all mine and all yours, and you know Sally doesn't mean a thing to me. Jane, I love you!"

But Jane didn't hear his last declaration. She had pulled away in simple horror, turned, and run.

"Jane," Howard said again, really believing himself, "Jane, I love you!"

Jane was gone.

After a long moment he heaved himself into his chair, snuffling and hiccuping. He unfolded a neat, white handkerchief and wiped his eyes. Then he lifted the telephone, dialed a number, and said into it tremulously, "Oh, Mother, tell me what to do. . . ."

Sally was nowhere to be seen, nor did Jane want to find her. Walking like a puppet, she went back to her car, and sat inside. Then she drove home. She obeyed all the signs, made all the proper signals, even smiled and waved at some people on the street. She remembered nothing. In her own driveway she stared at the door latch, unseeing. At last, when cold began to penetrate the haze, she pushed the latch, opened the door and got out.

She stood ankle deep in the snow, fishing for her key, and realized dimly that night had come. The sky was a black diamond pricked with hard crystal stars. The fir trees wore ermine coats. The tall streetlamps turned the snowbanks into sparkling mica, and up and down the avenue the myriad elf lights, like fireflies, still heralded a Christmas three days past.

What am I going to do?

Go into the house, a strange voice inside her said, *and pack. You were going to pack—remember? Do it. You can't stay here. Staying here means seeing Howard again, and Sally, and you needn't do that; you can get an attorney to straighten out your affairs. Staying here means asking for friendship from people who are afraid of Howard. You needn't do that, either. Staying would be a foolish courage, leading nowhere. You've already been that route: nowhere.*

She lifted her face to the ebony sky and cried out silently. "But where do I go?"

Her heart ached for Limeberry, but that was no answer and she knew it. Limeberry was in the business of being nice; Karen and Tom were friends for money—each week a new batch of friends.

She was last week's batch.

Some other town then. It was as simple as that. Some other town, a motel, quiet, someplace where she could get her head together. Thank God she hadn't redeposited the rest of her two thousand dollars!

One step at a time, she told herself wearily. She unlocked the door and went inside.

As she was packing, the telephone began to ring. She froze. *Howard,* she thought, and her heart began to drum. *He can't believe I'm through. His ego won't let him believe.*

Dumb Jane. That's what Sally had called her, and it was an uncomfortable truth. Dumb Jane.

Even her mother had thought so. Looking back, she could see it—always sheltered, always babied, never allowed to make her own decisions.

Damn it! Telephone, stop! Stop, I say! It stopped. "Thank you," said Jane out loud and laughed. It was better than crying.

She turned down the thermostat, picked up her suitcase, and went out the door. It seemed to be getting colder. Her feet crunched in the snow as she put the luggage in the trunk, and came around to the driver's side.

Damn. The tea set was still in the car.

Grimly she toted it back up on the porch, balanced it on one knee, and unlocked the door again. She had a satisfying vision of Mother Van Tassel and her long table of expensive wedding gifts, all to be returned. With explanations.

She put the tea set on the table with no regrets, and as an added fillip, pulled off Howard's diamond ring, dropping it in the sugar basin.

Suddenly the spate of amused detachment began to leave her. She started to shake, and her mouth set hard to stifle the sounds that wanted to come out.

She would not give in! Not to anything!

The telephone rang again.

Jane turned to run. Then she thought, *Whoa! I am twenty-two years old. I am not a child.*

Her heart thumping, swallowing hard, she put out her hand for the receiver and said, "Hello."

There was a pay phone sound. Then another, strange, rattling noise. Through it all, Tom Nelson's deep voice said coldly, "Jane?"

She sat down because her knees would not hold her. Almost

whispering, she answered, "Yes." Behind that single word were a thousand jumbled words all crying, *Tom, come get me. Tom, I need you. . . .*

But none of that could be said. She didn't want sympathy. Sympathy would trap them both. Sympathy would make a mockery of something they might have had. Sympathy would put her in Tom's bed where she wanted to be—but not the right way. Her life was messed up enough without that.

"You sound strange," he was saying. "Do you have a cold?"

"Yes. That is—sort of."

"How the hell do you sort of have a cold? You either do or you don't."

Why was he snapping at her? "All right!" she snapped back. "I have a cold!"

"Then I hope you're smart enough to get a shot for it. You sound awful."

"Well, I'm sorry!" This was ridiculous. She swallowed, and asked, "How's Karen?"

"She's fine. You left some stuff behind. She's mailing it."

"Oh, Thank her for me when you see her. When are you going back?"

"Tomorrow morning." He seemed to hesitate. There was a strained silence. Her heart twisted inside her, longing for him. But he was three hundred miles away. It may as well be as far as the moon.

She heard the rattling sound in the phone again, and a cowboy yell. Then someone called, "Get me another beer, Murphy." Through it he said stiffly, "Anyway—many happy returns—or whatever you say when someone gets married."

But I'm not! She almost said it out loud. She would have, except that he went on casually. "Good luck. If anyone ever needed a keeper, it's you."

"Good-bye, Tom," she said and hung up before she began to cry.

Why had he even bothered to call?

She was halfway back to the car when it hit like a bolt of

182

lightning: the rattling sound, and the cowboy yell—pinball machines! Pinball machines and a bartender named Murphy.

Tom Nelson was not three hundred miles away! He was at the truck stop on the edge of town!

She stumbled and almost fell full length in the snow. Her shoes filled and she tore one stocking, but she didn't care. *Please, dear God, let me get there before he leaves!*

It was a very cold night. The highways were slick, and the truck stop was a forest of steaming, grinding diesels, all purring away while their drivers refreshed themselves inside. Jane's car slithered to a halt. She was half out when an attendant said, "Hey, lady, you can't leave it there; you'll get flattened. Pull 'er around the pumps."

"All right! All right, I will, but—have you seen a—a man—not a trucker—tall, dark hair, tanned—" He grinned and she felt her face crimson. "Please—it's important!"

He nodded over his shoulder toward the car wash. "There was one over there in the third bay—a rental. Would that be it?"

"Maybe. I don't know. Where?"

"The third bay. See the white rear end sticking out?"

"Thank you."

She sprinted off like a deer through the half-frozen slush. He watched her go, sighing. Dames. How did some of those guys do it, anyway?

The car was clean and steaming, but the bay was empty. Beyond was a glass-doored entrance with two signs: TO MOTEL and TO CAFÉ.

Jane hopped through the slush, skidded on the steps, and grabbed at the door to keep herself from falling. It came open, dropping her idiotically to one knee in three inches of ice water, wrenching one shoulder, and shocking her out of her numbness.

Carefully she got up and, grimacing, smoothed her hair, straightened her coat, and forced her breathing to slow down. She might be a first-class idiot, but she needn't look like one.

Heat from the corridor came out in a wave. She wiped her feet on a track-darkened mat and glanced around. There was no one by the cigarette machine, or down the hall to the motel. The café, then. *Please let him be in the café.* She could enter casually, be so surprised . . .

In an alcove by the cigarette machine stood a tall man in a leather coat—a tall, tanned man. He was ardently occupied in an explicit and volatile embrace with a sleazily dressed young woman who had a viselike grip on his head and was squealing, "Oh, you wicked man! Oh, Tommy!"

Jane stopped dead. Then, like an automaton, she took one step backward. Then another and another. She felt the door behind her, opened it, and fled.

This time there were no tears. Dead people don't cry.

Two truckers in cowboy hats emerged from the service station, their shoulders hunched against the cold, their breaths trailing white plumes. Talking and laughing, they came toward her. She didn't want to meet them. Blindly she turned aside between two enormous, chugging trucks. The wind, down the valley of their towering sides, was knife-edged, taking her own breath away. She turned again, slipped, and almost fell, grabbing at a cold, chrome bumper, seeing nothing but rows of steaming diesels. She turned a third time, and found still more trucks.

It was like a nightmare. She was lost in eighteen-wheelers; she had no idea where she was. Senselessly she began to run, bumping into things half seen in the semi-darkness, almost sobbing, wanting only to find her own car, and get out of this horrible place.

She turned another corner, careened into an upright post, clung to it and, looking wildly around, recognized, thank God, the carwash bays. And there was the café and the pumps.

Her banging heart quieted. She rubbed at teary eyes with half-frozen hands, pulled up the hood of her coat, and buried her stiff hands deep in her pockets. She walked on cold, leaden feet toward her Buick.

"Jane!" called a deep voice.

Stunned, she turned. Tom stood by his car. The light from fluorescent tubing flashed down on his dark head, turning it blue, then black, then blue again. His hands were jammed into the side pockets of a light Windbreaker. He seemed to need a shave, and his eyes were mere slits beneath drawn brows. But it was Tom! It was Tom!

"You don't have a leather coat," she said in a whisper.

"What?"

His voice sounded harsh. He reached out, grabbed her arm, and pulled her into the half shelter of the car-wash bay.

She repeated, almost dazed, "You don't have a leather coat."

He dropped her arm and stepped back, scowling. "Of course I don't have a leather coat," he said. "I can't afford a leather coat! I possibly can't even afford the rental bill on this heap I'm driving."

"Then why did you come?"

"I didn't come! I'm just passing through, and I stopped to be nice and say congratulations to a girl getting married tomorrow. Which I did say. On the phone. Right? Right. Unless you want it in writing."

The euphoria, the fantastic, singing, dancing, rejoicing sounds in her head when she realized it hadn't been Tom Nelson in the corridor—all those feelings died in the steady gaze of his cold gray eyes.

Just passing through.

What an idiot you are, Jane Doorn. What a lovesick dummy!

"Oh," she said and nodded. Her smile was stiff, but determinedly bright. "Well. I was just having my gas tank filled. I'll see if it's done. Nice meeting you again, Tom."

"I'll buy you a cup of coffee."

"Oh, no," she said quickly. "I'd better get on. They—he—I'm expected. There's a—a party."

"Then I'll be on my way. After I kiss the bride."

His last words caught her unprepared. They were so quiet. Her hands flew from her pockets, but not soon enough. Her hood fell back as he scooped her up in his arms. Her startled eyes saw only his hard mouth coming closer before he closed them with his kisses, warmed the cold tip of her nose, then hungrily possessed her own mouth until she clung to him without the will or strength to let go.

It was Tom himself who stopped, dropping her from him suddenly.

Hurt him! a voice inside her said. *Hurt him, as he's hurt you!*

"You haven't changed!" she said. "Still trying to pick it up on the road, aren't you?"

"Nor have you changed, sweetheart," his harsh voice answered. "You're still answering the call!"

Her face flamed, but what she almost said never came out. Instead they both turned. The attendant reached past and turned off a dripping water tap.

"There we go," he said cheerfully. "Got to watch those things. 'Nough ice around here as 'tis. Glad you found the guy you were looking for, lady."

As he left, Tom turned back. Jane stood frozen. In an unbelieving, incredulous voice he asked, "Why were you looking for me?"

"I—I wasn't. He's mistaken. I told you," she said, suddenly desperate. "I came out to get gas—"

"You left a party with your esteemed fiancé—a pre-nuptial party at that—to come out to a dirty truck stop for gas?"

She clenched her fists. "It's none of your damned business what I do!"

"I'm making it my business!"

"You've no right!"

"I'm taking the right!"

"You can't do that!"

"The hell I can't!"

She gave a small sob of total despair and turned to run. He caught her hand. Her hair was ruffled across her forehead, and in the dim light her eyes looked like wet, purple pansies. "Please let me go," she said in a very small voice.

"Will you listen?"

"What is there to say?"

"I love you."

The hoarse sound was her breath catching. But she didn't believe him—he could see she didn't believe him, and the arm inside his hand had tensed.

186

"Damn," he said. "What else *is* there to say? I love you. I'm not just passing through. I'm here because I couldn't stay away, because I couldn't let you marry that bonehead until I knew how you felt. God knows, you may not be any better off with me than with him. I can't make any promises except—except that my first, last, and total commitment is to you, Jane. It's all I have. Is it enough?"

He dropped his hand. She stood alone, her feet in slush and her shoulders rounded against the mean blade of the icy wind. She looked at him, and she didn't see Limeberry with its warm white sands, or an end to trudging to work at Elbert Electronics, or the sweet song of revenge for Howard Van Tassel's petty, greedy scheming.

She saw Tom Nelson, hunched and shivering against the cold, wearing an inadequate jacket. Tom Nelson who said he loved her. Tom Nelson waiting for an answer from her as though it was the most important thing in his world.

She let out her breath in a sigh. "It's enough," she said. She took one step toward him, but he met even that, catching her up in his arms, not kissing her, not talking, just holding her.

A sudden cacophony of diesel horns, a spatter of applause and flashing headlights effectively broke the spell.

"Good God!" Tom said and laughed. Jane buried her suddenly bright pink face in his coat, but she was giggling. Both of them realized at the same time that a well-lighted car-wash bay was a very public place.

"Hey, Mac," called a friendly voice, "if you need a warmer place to make out, you can borrow my sleeper cab!"

Tom shook his head, grinning. To the tousled head against his shoulder he said, "Warmer is a fine idea. Like Limeberry. Tomorrow. Where's your car?"

"On the other side of the pumps."

"Do you have to go home?"

"I am home."

Her quiet voice shook him. "I love you!" he said.

He kissed her once more, took three bows, and they drove away.

LOOK FOR NEXT MONTH'S
CANDLELIGHT ECSTASY ROMANCES™:

Love—the way you want it!

Candlelight Romances

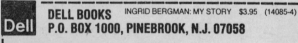

Dell Bestsellers

☐ **FEED YOUR KIDS RIGHT**
    by Lendon Smith, M.D. $3.50 (12706-8)
☐ **THE RING** by Danielle Steel $3.50 (17386-8)
☐ **INGRID BERGMAN: MY STORY**
    by Ingrid Bergman and Alan Burgess $3.95 (14085-4)
☐ **THE UNFORGIVEN**
    by Patricia J. MacDonald $3.50 (19123-8)
☐ **WHEN THE WIND BLOWS** by John Saul $3.50 (19857-7)
☐ **RANDOM WINDS** by Belva Plain $3.50 (17158-X)
☐ **SOLO** by Jack Higgins $2.95 (18165-8)
☐ **THE CRADLE WILL FALL**
    by Mary Higgins Clark $3.50 (11476-4)
☐ **LITTLE GLORIA . . . HAPPY AT LAST**
    by Barbara Goldsmith $3.50 (15109-0)
☐ **THE HORN OF AFRICA** by Philip Caputo ...$3.95 (13675-X)
☐ **THE OWLSFANE HORROR** by Duffy Stein ..$3.50 (16781-7)
☐ **THE SOLID GOLD CIRCLE**
    by Sheila Schwartz $3.50 (18156-9)
☐ **THE CORNISH HEIRESS**
    by Roberta Gellis $3.50 (11515-9)
☐ **AMERICAN BEAUTY** by Mary Ellin Barret $3.50 (10172-7)
☐ **ORIANA** by Valerie Vayle $2.95 (16779-5)
☐ **EARLY AUTUMN** by Robert B. Parker $2.50 (12214-7)
☐ **LOVING** by Danielle Steel $3.50 (14657-7)
☐ **THE PROMISE** by Danielle Steel $3.50 (17079-6)

At your local bookstore or use this handy coupon for ordering:

Dell | **DELL BOOKS**
P.O. BOX 1000, PINEBROOK, N.J. 07058

Please send me the books I have checked above. I am enclosing $_____
(please add 75¢ per copy to cover postage and handling). Send check or money
order—no cash or C.O.D.'s. Please allow up to 8 weeks for shipment.

Mr/Mrs/Miss _____

Address _____

City _____ State/Zip _____